D0455135

SPY PENGUINS

GOLDEN EGG

SAM HAY

Illustrated by MAREK JAGUCKI

FEIWEL AND FRIENDS · NEW YORK

A FEIWEL AND FRIENDS BOOK
An imprint of Macmillan Publishing Group, LLC
120 Broadway, New York, NY 10271

Our books may be purchased in bulk for promotional, educational, or business use. Please
contact your local bookseller or the Macmillan Corporate and Premium Sales Department
at (800) 221-7945 ext. 5442 or by email at MacmillanSpecialMarkets@macmillan.com.

Library of Congress Cataloging-in-Publication Data is available.

ISBN 978-1-250-18863-2 (hardcover) / ISBN 978-1-250-18864-9 (ebook)

Book design by Trisha Previte

Feiwel and Friends logo designed by Filomena Tuosto

First edition, 2020

1 3 5 7 9 10 8 6 4 2

mackids.com

FOR MUM AND WOOLLY MAMMOTH
MAVERICKS EVERYWHERE

GOLDEN EGG

Secret Agent 00Zero (also known as Jackson to his mom) grabbed a handful of hair and used it to haul himself up the side of the woolly mammoth. "Whoa!" he said. "It's like sitting on the roof of a monster-truck sled!"

"Yeah, I wish we could bring it to school on Monday for Snow-and-Tell!" his best friend, Quigley, said, climbing up next to him. Quigley (also known as Secret Agent Q to Jackson) pressed another button on the controller he was holding, and the mammoth

swished its tail and flapped its ears. "This would make *the* best undercover spy vehicle!"

"*Undercover* spy vehicle?" Jackson couldn't believe his feathers. "Uh, I think enemy agents might see us coming—watch it!" Jackson ducked as the mammoth flicked back its trunk and nearly knocked him off.

"Wow!" Quigley breathed. "So lifelike!"

Jackson smiled nervously and held on tighter. When Quigley had mentioned the idea of visiting the museum on Saturday morning to help his crazy inventor cousin, Sunny, with his new mechanical-dinosaur exhibits, Jackson had gotten *that* feeling. The disaster-waiting-to-happen feeling he always got when Sunny was involved. Sunny's inventions were even scarier than Quigley's! Jackson still had the red patches from the automatic face-washer flipper his mom had bought off Sunny a few weeks ago. It dangled down on a long arm from the bathroom ceiling and was supposed to lightly wipe your face while you brushed your beak. But one morning it had wrapped itself around Jackson's body like a giant squid tentacle and kept scrubbing his face until he'd managed to fight it off.

Now, the mammoth tossed its head again and let out a loud bellow. Several little hatchlings who'd been looking at the mammoth squealed and ran to their parents.

"Er, Quigley," Jackson whispered, "I think the mammoth is scaring people. Maybe we should wait for Sunny?"

"Nah!" Quigley grinned. "Sunny said we could try it out while he fetched a snack. And it's so neat!" He gave the lever on the control another wiggle, and the mammoth thudded its tusks on the floor. "It actually behaves just like a real live woolly mammoth."

"Yeah, that's the problem!" Jackson said as more visitor penguins backed away from their plinth.

Quigley pressed a different button on the remote. "Maybe I can make it quieter."

"That's not the make-it-quieter button!" Jackson gasped as the mammoth lunged forward.

The mammoth was now lumbering off its plinth, swinging its trunk and shaking its head. A couple of teenagers screamed. Some dad penguins with eggs on their toes backed away. A tiny hatchling in a stroller started to cry.

"Quigley!" Jackson shouted. "You've got to stop this thing."

"I'm trying!" Quigley waggled the control lever in every direction. "It isn't responding."

The mammoth let out a roar, its giant tusks swaying. Then suddenly it shot forward.

"Watch out!" Jackson shouted. "We're going to hit that—"

WOOLLY RHINOCEROS

"Woolly rhino," Jackson muttered.

The rhino dino's bones collapsed in a heap. But still the mammoth wasn't done. It reared up on its back legs, bellowing like a startled walrus and lurching from side to side.

"Uh-oh! I'm sli-i-i-ding!" Jackson scrabbled to stay on top. *Got to hold on. Can't fall off!* He racked his brain for some secret-agent survival trick that might help . . . *Of course! The Sticky Starfish Technique!* He spread his body

out across the mammoth's back like a starfish on a rock, willing every one of his feathers to sucker onto the creature's fur. Uncle Bryn, who was a real-life secret agent with the FBI (the Frosty Bureau of Investigation), said the Sticky Starfish Technique was perfect for surviving being shoved down the side of a building. Or was it an iceberg? Or maybe a garbage chute or— "Ahhhh!"

Crash! The mammoth smashed into another giant model—a huge skeleton of a cave bear that was under construction. Bones scattered. Scaffolding collapsed and clouds of dust filled the air.

"Wow, dudes!" Jackson heard a voice from below. He glanced down and saw Quigley's cousin, Sunny, holding a large krill burger. "It's like the clash of the mighty prehistoric beasts!" Sunny laughed. "Mammoth 1, Cave Bear 0! Hey, cuz," he added to Quigley, "toss

me the remote control. I think you put it in
fighter mode."

And seconds later, with the controller back
in Sunny's flippers, the mammoth stopped
moving. "It's a wild ride, huh?" Sunny looked
proudly up at his creation. "But maybe the
museum dudes need to give it more space."

Yeah, Jackson thought, *like a whole
flipper-ball pitch!*

"What is going on in here?" An angry-looking security guard came running into the hall. Jackson froze. For a second he thought it was his mom—she wore a similar uniform for her job at the department store. Then he remembered she wasn't working today; she was outside somewhere, doing an activity with the Egg, Jackson's soon-to-be-sibling. Jackson breathed a sigh of relief. If his mom had seen him dangling off the back of a nine-foot mammoth, she'd definitely have reached Hammerhead on her Shark Scale of Crossness!

Sunny smiled at the guard. "Oh, sorry, ma'am, we've just had a slight malfunction."

"A *slight* malfunction?" The security guard rolled her eyes, then plucked a walkie-talkie out of her belt and spoke into it. "Would the bone-building team please report to the dino hall?" she said. "Two of the skeletons have collapsed. And can you ask the janitor to fetch a ladder?" She looked up at Jackson and Quigley. "A very *long* ladder!" She put the walkie-talkie back in her belt. "What are you two doing up there?"

Jackson was about to explain how he and Quigley had been helping Sunny by safety-testing the new exhibits when he heard something bleep inside his backpack. "Quigley!" he hissed. "Listen!"

Quigley's eyes sparkled, and a huge smile spread across his beak. "The FBI radio transmitter!"

They'd found it weeks ago, when Jackson's Uncle Bryn had lost it in a pond at the city aquarium. Before they could return it to him, Uncle Bryn had gotten a replacement, so the boys had decided it was probably okay to keep it. After all, if Jackson and Quigley wanted to prove to the FBI they had the skills required to become junior agents, they needed to keep up with every secret mission.

Jackson reached into his backpack and pulled the transmitter out.

Calling all agents, calling all agents! A master criminal has escaped from Rookeryville Jail. All agents respond!

Jackson felt his feathers stand on end; his Adventure Detectors were maxing out. "It's another mission!" he whispered. "Come on, Agent Q, this is our chance to show the FBI they need us. We've got to find that escaped criminal. Let's do this!"

They didn't wait for the ladder. Instead they shimmied down the mammoth's trunk and raced for the doors.

"We'll be back soon," Quigley called to his cousin. But Sunny already had his head inside the mammoth's belly, tweaking its control panel.

"I wonder who the escaped criminal is," Jackson whispered.

"I hope it's not Blow Frost!" Quigley shuddered. "He looked so mad when they took him off to jail."

Jackson and Quigley had recently been responsible for catching a super-baddie named Blow Frost, who had tried to take over the town with mind-controlling ice cream. Uncle Bryn had very nearly gotten framed for Blow Frost's crimes. If it hadn't been for Jackson and Quigley, he would have been in jail by now.

"Well, we've caught Blow Frost once," Jackson said, puffing out his chest feathers, "so we can do it again. Come on. We'll cycle over to Rookeryville Jail and find out what's going on."

But as they dashed through the doors into the main hall of the museum, Jackson froze; a familiar figure was coming toward them, and this time there was no mistake.

"Mom!" Jackson squeaked.

Marina Rockflopper smiled. Then sneezed. Then sneezed again. "Sorry, boys," she said, blowing her beak on a large spotty hanky.

"Are you okay?" Jackson asked. "You look kind of sick."

She nodded. "Yeah, I think I'm coming down with your dad's—achoooo!"

"Flu?" Jackson suggested. Dad had been in bed for two days with a runny beak, a high fever, and aching feathers. Now it looked like his mom had caught it, too.

"That's why I came to find you," she said. "I'm so relieved you're here. When you said you were coming to the museum to help Sunny, I wondered whether it was really a cover story for another crazy scheme to join the FBI."

"Ha! Of course not!" Jackson laughed nervously and glanced at Quigley. His buddy's face had turned red and his beak was opening like he was about to say something incriminating. Jackson stepped in front of him so his mom couldn't see. Whenever he had to fib, Quigley turned into a wibbly, wobbly jellyfish—especially with Jackson's mom: Marina Rockflopper could suck the truth out of a penguin faster than a frost vacuum on max power.

Jackson's mom swung her backpack off her shoulder and began rummaging inside. "I've decided to go home to bed," she said. "Jackson, I need you to look after the Egg for me. Here, can you take it, please?"

"What?" Jackson stared at his soon-to-be-sibling. "B-b-but I can't! What about Finola?"

"Your sister's at band camp, remember?" His mom handed him the Egg. "I'm so sorry, Jackson, but I really don't feel—achoooo!" She dabbed her beak with her handkerchief and groaned. "Oh, my head hurts."

Jackson's shoulders sagged. "Sure. Of course I'll help. You go home and rest."

"Thank you." Jackson's mom blew her nose. "Remember to keep an eye on the Egg, because it's started rolling off. This morning I nearly put it out with the trash. Good thing I looked inside the garbage bag."

"Oh, I can help you with that, Mrs. Rock-flopper." Quigley pulled open his backpack. "See, I invented this awesome new tracker patch. It looks like a Band-Aid. You stick it on your valuables and you can track them on your phone and your watch. Look, I'll show you. You

just put it on like this"—he reached over and stuck a small blue patch on the Egg—"and then you can track it on an app on your iceWatch."

"That's great, honey," Jackson's mom said with a smile. "You use this clever Band-Aid thingy to help Jackson look after the Egg for me, okay? And here's some extra allowance for snacks," she added, pushing some money into Jackson's flipper. "You're going to need lots of energy. Today's the Rookeryville Golden Egg Games, and, Jackson, I'm going to need you to take my place and compete with the Egg."

"The Golden Egg what?" Jackson frowned. The name rang bells, but he couldn't quite remember why.

"I told you about it at breakfast." His mom shook her head. "I swear you never listen. The contest is held every ten years. And whoever wins—either as Egg or Egg's guardian—gets their name on the Rookeryville Golden Egg Cup, and then they can become mayor someday."

Jackson shrugged. "I don't want to be mayor." *I want to join the FBI*, he wanted to add but didn't because his mom thought being a secret agent was far too dangerous.

"Well, you don't have to be mayor," Mom said. "But the Egg might like to someday. 'Mayor Rockflopper' has got quite a ring to it, don't you think?" She blew her beak again, then picked up her bag. "The contest is taking place on the grounds of the museum, so you don't have to go far. You just need to register. Thanks, boys. I'm so grateful. Oh, and Jackson, make sure the Egg gets plenty of rest. Pop it in your backpack when it's not doing activities. It's close to hatching, and it needs lots of sleep. Oh, and also, watch out for the blizzard storm that's forecast for the afternoon. Make sure the Egg stays nice and cozy. Okay, you got all that? Good!" she said without waiting for a reply. "I'll see you later."

"But, Mom—" Jackson called as his mom shuffled away. "I don't even know what happens in the Golden Games!"

"Look! It's working!" Quigley said, showing Jackson his watch. "That flashing light shows that the Egg is here with us, in the museum."

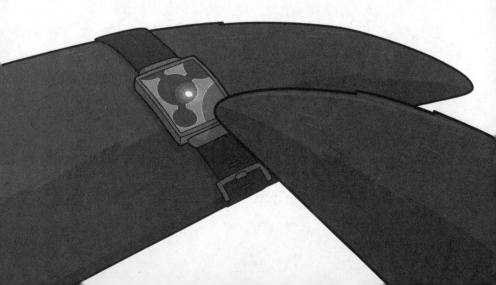

"Unfortunately!" Jackson muttered. He looked at the Egg and sighed. Shell-sitting was not part of his plan. How were they going to catch an escaped criminal with an egg to look after?

"**S**o what's this **Golden Egg Challenge** thing all about?" Jackson asked as they shuffled outside to register. "Maybe it won't take long and we can still join the search for the escaped criminal."

Quigley peered at his icePhone. "Well, according to the Golden Egg Games' webbedsite, it's a whole day of contests to judge bravery, stamina, and egg-caring aptitude, whatever that means."

"A whole day!" Jackson groaned.

The courtyard outside was a sea of activity.

Dozens of official-looking penguins in T-shirts that read EGG-CITED TO HELP! were setting up tables and benches. Behind them, Jackson could see a large area had been sectioned off with climbing frames, benches, and high ropes.

"Oh, wow!" Quigley nudged Jackson. "Look! That must be the Golden Egg Cup."

Four large penguins walked past carrying

an enormous glass case. Inside was an egg-shaped trophy, glinting and sparkling in the daylight.

"See all the names carved on it?" Quigley said. "I guess they must belong to previous mayors."

"Well, I can tell you one name that won't be going on it," Jackson muttered. "Mine! Hey—what's happening over there?"

Three large black ice-sleds had just pulled up outside the museum, and several serious-looking penguins in dark glasses were piling out.

"The FBI!" Jackson whispered. "What are they doing here? Wait—there's Uncle Bryn. Let's go find out."

Uncle Bryn smiled nervously as they raced toward him. He glanced over to see if his boss, Senior Agent Frost-Flipper, was watching. She wasn't the friendliest sort of penguin, especially where Jackson and Quigley were concerned. But she was headed straight for the museum. "Hi, boys. What are you doing here?" Uncle Bryn asked.

"We're egg-sitting for Mom," Jackson said, holding up his soon-to-be-sibling. "She wasn't feeling too good, so I'm taking her place at the Golden Egg Games."

"Oh yeah. I heard that was today," Uncle Bryn said. "Well, good luck, Jackson. And you, too, little one," he added, patting the Egg. He went to follow his boss into the museum, but Jackson stepped in front of him.

"Are you on a mission?" Jackson asked. "Are you looking for someone—here in the museum?"

Uncle Bryn held up his flippers. "Now, Jackson, you know I can't talk about FBI business."

"Please." Jackson dropped his voice to a

whisper. "We won't say anything. You know you can trust us."

Quigley nodded and made a beak-zipping motion with his flipper.

Uncle Bryn shuffled uncomfortably. "I really shouldn't say . . ." He sighed. "But you guys did help me out with that whole Blow Frost business, so I guess I owe you." He looked around to make sure his colleagues weren't watching, but the other agents had already followed their boss inside the museum. "We're looking for an escaped criminal," he said, his voice a whisper now. "A jewel thief named Icejob."

Jackson glanced at Quigley. *Wow*, he mouthed.

"Icejob escaped over the wall of Rookeryville Jail this morning," Uncle Bryn said. "He's an ace climber, as well as the best jewel thief in the city. So until he's caught, the FBI is staking out all of Rookeryville's most precious jewels."

"And there's a jewel here?" Jackson asked. "At the museum?"

Uncle Bryn nodded. "It's about to go on display. It's called the Ice Dragon's Eye."

"Oh, I heard about that," Quigley said. "It was on TV. It's the biggest sapphire ever found."

"Yeah, and it's a very rare color," Uncle Bryn said. "Almost clear, like glass. So we've got to make sure Icejob doesn't get his flippers on it. He's a master of disguise, which means he could look like anyone—even you, Jackson." Uncle Bryn smiled. "Now, I've got to go. Remember, don't tell anyone about this, okay?"

"Sure!" Jackson gave Uncle Bryn a flippers-up. "And if we see anything suspicious, we'll let you know."

"Um—maybe not," Uncle Bryn said. "Your mom got pretty mad at me the last time you got involved in FBI business. It's probably best if you two just go enjoy the Games, okay?"

Jackson waited until Uncle Bryn had gone, then he snorted. "Not get involved? As if! Come on! Let's get back inside the museum. Mom will never know. I'll just say I didn't win the egg trophy thing."

But Quigley didn't reply. He was looking over Jackson's shoulder. "I think that lady in the pink hat is waving at you."

"Huh?" Jackson glanced over. "Oh no! Mrs. Heckle-Flipper!"

Doreen Heckle-Flipper was his mom's best friend and officially the chattiest penguin on the planet. When Doreen Heckle-Flipper started talking, time stood still.

"Quick!" Jackson hissed. "If she spots us, there's no way we'll be able to help the FBI. Pretend you haven't seen her. Make for the museum! RUN!"

"**J**ackson! *Jackson!*" **Mrs. Heckle-Flipper** raced after them. "*JACKSON ROCK-FLOPPER!* Stop right there, young man!"

Jackson skidded to a halt on the museum steps. "Oh, hi, Mrs. Heckle-Flipper. I didn't see you there."

"Aren't you supposed to be at the Golden Egg Games?" she puffed.

Jackson shrugged. "Um—I was just looking for the registration desk."

"Well, you're going the wrong way!" Mrs. Heckle-Flipper smiled. "When I suggested to your mom that she go home to rest, what with her being so sick and all, not to mention the freezing blizzard that's forecast, I promised to keep an eye out for you. Come on, I'll show you the way; I've just registered my egg." She pointed to a small, speckled egg in a carry pack on her front. "Isn't it growing?"

"Sure," Jackson mumbled.

"And, oh my!" Mrs. Heckle-Flipper said, peering at Jackson's soon-to-be-sibling. "I think you're going to be a big brother *very* soon. You guys will have so much fun looking after a hatchling, won't you?"

"I guess." Jackson looked longingly at the museum doors, then followed her toward the registration table.

"So this must be your first Games," Mrs. Heckle-Flipper said. "Are you excited? Because I know I am. And so is Cutie-Flipper."

"Cutie-Flipper?" Quigley asked.

Mrs. Heckle-Flipper smiled. "That's what I call my egg."

Jackson tried hard not to make a *yuck* face.

"You know, I think your mom had a pet name for you when you were just an egg, Jackson." Mrs. Heckle-Flipper frowned. "I'm trying to remember what it was."

Jackson coughed. "Um—I don't think—"

"Sweet-Beak!" Mrs. Heckle-Flipper interrupted. "That's what she called you."

Quigley's eyes widened. "Sweet-Beak?"

Jackson glared at him.

Mrs. Heckle-Flipper nodded. "Because before you hatched, you used to tap-tap-tap on the inside of your shell with your sweet little beak." She beamed at him. "Cute, huh?"

Jackson wished the ground would swallow him whole, hungry-whale style. He cleared his throat. "Um—I think this is where we register . . . I'll join the line now. Thanks for your help."

"No problem," Mrs. Heckle-Flipper said. "My and your mom's other friends will be over here. We'll ALL be watching, so just holler if you need us. Oh, and Jackson, if you get chilly when that blizzard blows in this afternoon, just give me a wave, because I've got lots of spare woolly hats and scarves you can borrow. I always come prepared!" She smiled, then shuffled off to join a group of parents standing in a huddle.

"This is a nightmare." Jackson groaned.

"How are we going to escape from the Games with the Mom Squad watching us?"

"We could try a distraction technique," Quigley said.

Distraction techniques were the latest chapter of the *Secret Agent Handbook* they'd been studying: how to escape from your enemy by creating a diversion. The book's helpful suggestions included releasing an angry octopus into a crowded room, hiring a penguin with circus skills (fire-eater or juggler was best), or creating a bad stink. So far they'd only tried the smell technique. During the last math test at school, they'd "released" some of Jackson's dad's favorite stinky blue cheese, and Miss Chalk-Feather, their teacher, had definitely been distracted. Unfortunately, when she'd discovered the source of the smell, she'd been less distracted and had dished out a punishment that really stunk: litter-picking.

"Wait—I've got an idea," Quigley said, rummaging in his backpack.

"I hope so," Jackson muttered. "We're nearly at the front of the line and the Mom Squad is still 'eyes-on'!"

"Check this out!" Quigley held up a small fluffy ball. "Meet Chick-bot," he said, smoothing its feathers so Jackson could see its face. "It looks like a cute baby penguin, right?"

Jackson peered at the creature's stuck-on eyes, lopsided beak, and straggly fake feathers. "Um—I guess," he said, "if your cute baby penguin had somehow gotten stuck inside the washer-fluffer on the extra-hot rinse cycle."

Quigley grinned. "I made it for Sunny's new webbed-site. He's selling all sorts of cool remote-control gadgets now."

Jackson prodded the Chick-bot. "And you think this will distract the Mom Squad?"

"Sure! Haven't you ever been in a grocery store when a lost hatchling is calling for its mom? Everyone stops to help! Now watch this . . ." Quigley dropped the chick on the floor and hit a button on the tiny controller in his flipper.

"Ma-ma! Ma-ma!" The Chick-bot slowly rolled off through the crowd, heading straight for the Mom Squad.

Jackson watched it go. "I can't quite believe it, but, yeah, I think it is actually working. Look, they're not watching us now. They're cooing at the chick. Weird! Good work, Agent

Q. Come on, let's escape while they're 'eyes-off'!"

"Wait—" Quigley sniffed the air. "Do you smell burning?"

Just then there was a loud *pop!* and a tiny cloud of smoke drifted upward.

"Fire!" someone shouted. And instantly several organizer penguins came running, one armed with an extinguisher.

"Uh-oh!" Jackson said, peering through the crowds to see what was happening. "I think the Chick-bot just became an Ex-bot! Look, I can only see a beak and a few feathers left."

Quigley scratched his crest. "That's odd. I've never made one that caught fire before. I'd better tell Sunny before he sells any more."

"Name?" They'd reached the front of the line now, and an older penguin in thick glasses was peering up at Jackson from the desk. But before he could answer—

"Loser McLoser-Beak! That's his name!" shouted a familiar voice from behind them.

Jackson spun round and came flipper-to-flipper with— "Hoff Rockface!" he gasped. "Nightmare," he added under his breath.

"Ha!" Hoff snorted. "You aren't seriously entering the Golden Egg Games with THAT!" He prodded Jackson's soon-to-be-sibling, which wriggled crossly in reply.

Hoff was their worst enemy from school. He never missed a chance to ruin Jackson's day.

"THIS is what a champion egg looks like!" Hoff said, turning round to reveal a camo-colored carry-pack on his back, and strapped inside was an enormous egg that looked ready to hatch at any moment. "Meet my cousin.

And, cousin," he added, "meet Loser-McLoser-Beak and his Loser-Egg."

Jackson gritted his beak. "Get lost, Hoff!"

"For the last time," the penguin on the registration desk shouted. "WHAT'S YOUR NAME?"

"Um—I'm Jackson Rockflopper—and this is Egg Rockflopper."

She scribbled their names in the book in front of her. "Address?" she barked, not looking up.

"Number Five Surf-Spray Avenue." Jackson lowered his voice. "Only, I'm not sure if we're staying. See, I've got something else I've got to go and do and—"

"Too late!" The desk penguin glared up at him. "Once you're in the book, you're in the contest! Here's your number. Wear it around your neck." She handed Jackson a card attached to a string. "Next!" she shouted.

"Could this day get any worse?" Jackson sighed as they stepped out of the line. "I can't believe I'm stuck doing this dumb contest when we should be off catching Icejob."

"Wait—I've got it," Quigley said. "Just make sure you lose in the first round. Then you can tell your mom you entered."

"Genius idea!" Jackson looked longingly over at the museum. "Icejob could be in there right now, about to strike, about to steal the—"

"Hey, Loser-Beak!" Hoff shuffled over. "I bet my egg beats yours." Jackson ignored him. But Hoff pushed his big face right up close to Jackson's. "Hello? Did you hear me? There's no way a Rockflopper could ever beat a Rockface, because Rockfloppers have KRILL for brains!"

The Egg gave a cross little jiggle, and Jackson felt his feathers stand on end. He clenched his flippers, and a small earthquake of anger trembled through his belly. "Shut up, Hoff! Me and my egg could beat you and your egg any day—even if we were covered with itchy ice ants and soaked in slippy seaberry juice!"

"Really?" Hoff said. "Okay, challenge accepted!"

"What?" Jackson blinked. "Wait—no, I didn't mean—"

Hoff held up his flipper. "I ACCEPT your challenge. And just to make it more

interesting"—he paused—"now, let me think." A sneaky glint appeared in his eyes. "If you and your egg beat me, I'll be your servant after school for a whole week. But if you lose"—his eyes narrowed—"which you will, then you'll be MY servant! Deal?"

Jackson swallowed hard. He looked at the Egg. *Can we beat Hoff?* Jackson doubted it. *Hoff is always the fastest penguin on Flipper Track and Field Day. And anyway, we're planning to lose so we can go find Icejob.*

"Ha!" Hoff smirked at him. "I guess you're too scared to accept the challenge. Wait until I tell everyone at school."

"Fine!" Jackson said. "I accept."

"Awesome!" Hoff beamed. "You're going to be the best servant, Jackson. I'll make sure I find you a nice frilly apron and a pretty little cap to match. See ya!"

"Um—Jackson," Quigley said, when Hoff

had gone. "What happened to the plan to quit in the first round?"

Jackson puffed out his cheeks. "I know, but I couldn't let him say all that stuff about our Egg." He sighed. "I guess this is what's called being caught between a rock and a hard Rockface."

"**W**ould all remaining contestants please make their way to the start of the course!" boomed a loud speaker. "*The Golden Games have now begun!*"

As they shuffled over to the starting line, Jackson had a good look at the arena in front of them. "It must be some sort of obstacle course," he said, scanning the ramps, beams, and scramble nets. "But it seems WAY too easy. I mean, a hatchling could get over that frame."

"Hey, listen to this," Quigley interrupted,

peering at his icePhone. "I just did a webbed-search on Icejob. Guess what his real name is? . . . Custard Dorkfin!"

"What? No way!" Jackson chuckled. "Custard Dorkfin? Sheesh, I can see why he changed it to Icejob. What else did you find out about him? What does he look like?"

"That's the problem," Quigley said. "Apparently he looks just like a regular penguin. That's why he's so good at disguising himself."

Jackson stopped walking and glanced around. Maybe Icejob was here in the crowd somewhere, pretending to watch the Games while secretly preparing to go in and steal the Ice Dragon's Eye.

"But there's one thing that makes him stand out," Quigley added, looking at his cell screen again. "He's got a silver tattoo of an ice crystal on his beak."

"Really?" Jackson peered up at the teenage penguin next to him. Was that a tattoo on his beak? *Nah, just a zit.*

"Jackson?" He felt a tap on his back, and turned around.

"Oh, hi, Lily." Jackson smiled. Lily was their friend from school. She was super-smart and had helped them on previous missions. Jackson and Quigley thought she'd make a good FBI agent (with a bit of training from them, of course). But Lily wanted to be a rare-fish keeper at the aquarium, just like her dad.

"Are you guys taking part?" Lily asked.

Quigley shook his head. "Not me. Just Jackson and the Egg."

"What about you, Lily?" Jackson asked.

"I'm not competing. I'm a helper, see?" She pointed to her T-shirt. "But you should get over to the starting line, Jackson. The time trials are beginning."

"The what?" Jackson blinked at her.

"The first event is a knockout contest against the clock," Lily explained. "The fastest twelve penguins across the egg-stacle course go through to the second round. Everyone else is out of the Games!"

"What exactly is an egg-stacle course

anyway?" Jackson asked, following her toward the entrance gate.

"It's just like an obstacle race," Lily said. "But you have to go around with your egg balanced on your feet."

Jackson's eyes widened. So that was why the course looked easy. You had to do it with an egg on your toes. He glanced at his soon-to-be-sibling. "I've never carried it anywhere on my feet before."

"Don't worry," Quigley said. "Just imagine you're doing tricks with a flipper ball."

"But a flipper ball doesn't crack if I drop it." Jackson sighed. "These Games are stupid."

"No they're not!" Lily glared at him. "They're part of our heritage. Rookeryville penguins have been competing in the Games for more than a hundred years. Look, I'll show you." She picked up a leaflet from a nearby stand and opened it up.

The Legend of Rookeryville

MANY YEARS AGO A GROUP OF *PIONEER PENGUINS* SET OUT TO FIND A NEW PLACE TO SETTLE.

IT WAS A JOURNEY FILLED WITH *HAZARDS!*

EVENTUALLY THE GROUP FOUND A PLACE TO BUILD THEIR NEW HOME. BUT AS THEY UNPACKED, ONE OF THEIR EGGS *ROLLED AWAY.*

THE GROUP ALL JOINED THE SEARCH FOR THE EGG.

FINALLY, THEY FOUND IT.

BUT BEFORE THEY COULD RETURN TO THE PLACE THEY'D CHOSEN FOR THEIR NEW HOME, THE EGG BEGAN TO HATCH.

AS THEY WAITED FOR THE CHICK TO BE BORN, THEIR NEW HOME, FAR DOWN BELOW, SUDDENLY DISAPPEARED INTO A *GIANT ICE CRACK!*

IF IT HADN'T BEEN FOR THE EGG ROLLING AWAY, THEY'D ALL HAVE DIED!

THE CHICK WAS NAMED PIP ROOKERY, AND THE TOWN WAS CALLED *ROOKERYVILLE* IN HER HONOR.

WELCOME TO ROOKERYVILLE

THE PENGUINS ALSO DECIDED PIP SHOULD BECOME ITS FIRST *MAYOR* WHEN SHE GREW UP.

PIP'S BROKEN EGGSHELL WAS KEPT AS A REMINDER OF HOW SHE'D SAVED THEIR LIVES. IT WAS EVENTUALLY CAST INTO A *GOLDEN TROPHY.*

AND EVERY TEN YEARS, A *COMPETITION* IS HELD IN HER HONOR TO FIND A POTENTIAL MAYOR FOR THE TOWN—THUS, THE *GOLDEN EGG GAMES* WERE BORN.

THE GOLDEN EGG GAMES
—
THE EGG-ACT RULES:

BOTH THE EGG AND EGG'S GUARDIAN WILL HAVE THEIR NAMES ENGRAVED ON THE CUP.

ANYONE WHOSE NAME IS ENGRAVED ON THE CUP IS ELIGIBLE TO BECOME MAYOR.

ADULT PENGUINS CAN BECOME MAYOR ON THE DAY THEY WIN.

EGGS AND YOUNG PENGUINS CAN SERVE AS MAYOR WHEN THEY GROW UP.

THE MAYOR OF ROOKERYVILLE SERVES FOR TWO YEARS.

THE GAMES ARE HELD EVERY TEN YEARS.

IN BETWEEN GAMES, THE MAYOR OF ROOKERYVILLE IS ELECTED BY A VOTE.

"Cool story," Quigly said, peering over Jackson's shoulder. "So if you win the Games, either as an egg or the penguin looking after the egg, like Jackson, you can become mayor someday?"

"Yep, but you MUST have your name carved onto the cup as soon as you win," Lily explained.

"I guess that's why the cup is kept in a locked box," Jackson said, looking over at it sitting on the judges' table. "Just in case someone decides not to bother competing in the Games."

Lily nodded. "My mom said that nearly happened once—uh-oh." She glanced across at the starting line. "Quick, Jackson! If you don't hurry, you'll miss the time slots and be disqualified."

"No way!" Jackson shuffled after her. As they reached the entrance to the course, he handed the FBI radio transmitter to Quigley. "You'd better look after this," he whispered. "Just in case there are any updates on Icejob."

"Sure," Quigley replied, shoving it into his backpack.

In front of them, Hoff was just starting. He smirked at Jackson, then thundered away, somehow managing to keep his large egg perfectly balanced on his toes.

"He's probably glued it on," Quigley muttered.

Lily gave Jackson a gentle push forward. "Here's number thirty-seven," she called to a curly-crested penguin with a clipboard and whistle standing by the starting line.

The penguin nodded. "Put your egg on your toes, and remember, no holding it on with your flippers. The judges will be watching! Okay, are you ready?"

Jackson nodded. *This is it*, he thought. *Time to prove Rockfloppers are not losers!* "Come on, Egg," he whispered to his soon-to-be-sibling. "Let's do this!"

"Three, two, one." *Peep!* **The curly-crested** penguin blew her whistle, and Jackson shuffled off toward the first hurdle: a giant A-frame studded with spiky shells.

"Please don't roll off," Jackson whispered to the Egg as he began to climb. "Mom will go *Bull Shark* if I drop you in the first race."

The Egg seemed to have gotten the message. It leaned with him, left, then right as Jackson took each small, shuffling step. "Yow," Jackson muttered as his foot crushed a shell. He winced as he trod on another, then another.

Mustn't wobble the Egg! he told himself. *Must keep going!* And moments later— "Made it," he whispered as they scrambled down the other side.

"Okay, this one looks just like a seesaw," Jackson told the Egg as they approached the next egg-stacle: a long oar propped up on a barrel of fish. "You love seesaws, remember? It's just like the one in the park." Jackson began to climb, holding his flippers out to keep his balance. But as they reached the middle, the Egg seemed to get a bit overexcited and

began to jiggle. "Steady, steady . . ." Jackson gritted his beak as he teetered on the oar. "You've got to keep still!"

The Egg seemed to hear, and it froze rock-solid as Jackson flipped the oar to the other side of the barrel and they shuffled down.

"Go, Jackson!" he heard Quigley shout from the spectator area. "Awesome work!"

Jackson gave his buddy a wave, then bent down and patted the Egg. "See! We've got this," he whispered. "It's a piece of krill cake for us Rockfloppers."

They shuffled off down the path again, but as Jackson approached the next egg-stacle he skidded to a halt. "What the—" In front of him were a dozen spinning snow mushrooms. "Flying frost rats! What am I supposed to do here?"

"Hop across them!" Lily shouted from the crowd.

"Yeah, like you're rock-jumping over the icy river on Frostbite Ridge!" Quigley added.

"Gotcha!" Jackson crouched down and sprang onto the first mushroom. Then very nearly fell straight off. "Whoa!" *Can't let Hoff win!* Jackson shut his eyes as he spun around and around, trying to find his balance. The Egg wriggled against his toes. *What if it's getting scrambled inside its shell,* Jackson thought. *I've got to get off this, quick!* He opened his eyes, took a deep breath, then jumped onto the next mushroom. This time he didn't wait around. He hopped straight onto the next one, and then the next, springing from one to the other, until he landed on the ground at the end with a thump, blinking and swaying slightly.

"Run, Jackson!" Lily shouted. "Only the fastest penguins make it through to the next round!"

Head down, flippers tucked into his sides, Jackson zoomed on, speeding through a long icy tunnel, then ducking under a large net. He weaved in and out of a set of skinny ski poles and jumped over a snow ditch. "Wow! This is just like the secret agent exercises me and Quigley practice up on Frostbite Ridge," he puffed to the Egg. "When you hatch, I'll take you up there." *That's weird!* Jackson peered down at the Egg and frowned. *I never thought of you as an actual penguin before!*

"Quick, Jackson! It's the Surf Drop next," Lily called, pointing to a zigzagging flume of water shooting down a slope.

Jackson hesitated. He liked surfing. But he'd never done it downhill with an Egg on his toes before. "I hope you're waterproof," he whispered to the Egg as he grabbed a surfboard and launched into the flume. "Hold on

to your shell, little guy. This is going to get bump-y-y-y-y-y-y."

They zoomed down the flume, zigzagging left, then right, then—"Uh-oh! Steep drop ahea—!" Jackson closed his eyes as the board took off out of the water, then seconds later—

Smack!

They hit a pool at the bottom. Jackson thrashed his flippers up and down to keep his balance, his board wobbling violently in the surf. Somehow he managed to steer it out of the waves and glide to the side.

"Huh? We survived!" Jackson spluttered, hopping onto dry land. "I wasn't expecting that." The Egg jiggled up and down, *tap-tap-tapp*ing on its shell. "Hey—not so hard!" Jackson muttered. "You can't hatch now. We're not done yet!"

As he shuffled on to the next egg-stacle, Jackson felt a cloak of weariness fall over his feathers. "My l-l-legs feel like logs," he panted to the Egg. "I'm not sure I can make it."

The Egg began jiggling up and down again, bashing his legs.

"Okay, okay," Jackson puffed. "I get the message." He took a deep breath, gritted his beak, and stuck out his chin. "Let's do this!"

"Just one more egg-stacle to go!" Lily yelled. "It's the big one: the ice-blaster round!"

"The what?" Jackson gazed across the slippery rink ahead of him. *Ice sliding? But that's WAY too easy!* Then he spotted the catch: deep potholes dotted across the ice, making the course look like a giant pinball machine. Jackson shuddered. *And I guess I'm the ball!*

"Lean against the launch post, please," said a helper penguin, who had appeared next to him. The helper pointed to a curved piece of ice attached to a giant spring, which he was pulling back.

"Stand by," he said as Jackson leaned back. "Five . . . four . . . three . . ."

"Be careful!" Lily shouted. "There's a five-second time penalty for every hole you fall into!"

B-o-i-n-g! Jackson sprang forward, leaving his stomach behind. He whizzed across the ice, the wind in his crest, his feathers rippling, trying desperately to keep his toes straight so the Egg wouldn't fall off.

He steered left to avoid a pothole, then right, then hard left again. Up ahead he could see several penguins skidding and slipping, their flippers flapping as they tried to haul themselves out of holes. One of them was Hoff Rockface!

"Come on, Egg," he whispered. "We've got this!" He was starting to slow now; there were just sixty feet or so to go. The Egg leaned back into Jackson's legs, helping him keep his balance as they swerved to avoid another hole.

"Keep going, buddy!" Jackson heard Quigley shouting to him. "It's just like ice-sliding on Frostbite Ridge."

Head down, eyes staring at the ice, Jackson focused on every tiny bump and dip. Then, out of the corner of his eye, he spotted something up ahead: Hoff Rockface crouched on the ice. Jackson blinked. *Am I seeing things, or did Hoff just spill something?* A dark shape was now spreading out across the ice from Hoff toward him. Jackson tried to avoid it.

Too late! His feet hit the *something* and suddenly he was sliding and spinning and turning and twisting and twitching and jerking out of control and heading straight for the final set of giant potholes *and* the line of judges gathered there.

"S *top!"* **Jackson heard one of the judges** yell.

Flippers flapping, feet skidding, Jackson tried desperately to gain control. But the more he tried to stay upright, the more he spun. "Hold on tight!" he shouted to the Egg as they just missed a pothole. Jackson desperately racked his brain for something to save them. Then—*I've got it!* He suddenly remembered what Quigley had said about ice-sliding on Frostbite Ridge. Last time they'd been there, they'd tried a move from the *Secret*

Agent Handbook called the Slide and Glide Mind-Control Technique. According to the book, you could slide across a booby-trapped ice pond by shutting out the world, focusing on your breathing, and letting your body's natural abilities take over. It hadn't worked too well when they'd tried it: Jackson's natural ability had sent him smacking into a tree. But maybe this time . . .

Jackson clasped his flippers above his head, took a deep breath, and shut his eyes, imagining himself slipping across the ice, sailing over the potholes, gliding and sliding straight toward the finish line.

"T-u-n-d-r-aaaaaaa," he murmured as he breathed out, using the word the book recommended to help focus his mind. He took another breath, then—"T-u-n-d-r-aaaaaaaa," and he breathed out again.

"Wow, Jackson!" he thought he heard a tiny Lily-sounding voice say. "Awesome moves!" But it was too far away for him to hear properly, and anyway, he had to focus. *Blot out the world*, he reminded himself. "T-u-n-d-r-aaaaaaa," he breathed out again.

"Jackson! You can stop now, buddy. You made it back." This voice was louder, and it sounded more like Quigley's.

Mustn't get distracted, Jackson told himself. "T-u-n-d-r-aaaaaa . . ."

"*Jackson!*" The Quigley voice was right in his earhole now, and nudging him in the belly, too.

"Huh?" Jackson opened his eyes. He was at

the end of the course. Quigley was beaming at him. Lily was cheering. Wait—the whole world seemed to be cheering. Loads of spectator penguins were surrounding him, clapping and yelling and congratulating him. And the Egg was wriggling and jiggling wildly on his toes. "We made it?" Jackson's eyes opened wide. "Wow! *We made it!*"

"Well done, young man!" One of the judges shuffled over and patted him on the back. "When that other competitor accidentally dropped his juice, we thought you'd crash for sure." She frowned at Hoff, who was lurking in the crowd. She turned back to Jackson. "We've never seen anyone use such an unusual technique before. Some sort of yoga, was it?" She smiled. "Whatever it was, we've awarded you extra points for creative expression, which means—with no time penalties—you're at the top of the leaderboard!"

Jackson blinked in disbelief.

"Excuse me, can I have a few words, please."
A smart-looking penguin with a gelled-back
crest holding a microphone pushed through
the crowds. Behind him was a camera-penguin
with her lens on Jackson. "Hi, I'm Bill Feathers
from *Rookery Live*!" the well-groomed penguin
said in a smooth and impossibly deep voice.

"Oh yeah," Jackson squeaked. "I've seen
you on TV."

"Well *you're* the one on TV now," Bill

Feathers said, smiling at Jackson. Then he turned and looked down the lens of the camera. "This is Bill Feathers live at the Rookeryville Golden Egg Games, and I'm joined now by the penguin at the top of the leaderboard after round one." He turned back to Jackson. "What's your name, young man?"

"Um—Jackson Rockflopper," Jackson said, blinking in the bright light that shone from the camera. "And this is Egg Rockflopper," he added, pointing to his toes.

"And how does it feel to be top of the leaderboard, Jackson?" Bill Feathers asked.

"Um—great," Jackson mumbled. Somehow with the camera pointing at him all his words seemed to have melted.

"I'm guessing you've always wanted to be mayor of Rookeryville," Bill Feathers said.

"Well—um," Jackson was about to explain that he actually wanted to be a secret agent with the FBI, when suddenly he remembered that secret agents weren't allowed to talk about being secret agents, because then they stopped being secret agents, and became *not-very-secret-at-all* agents. "Um—I guess," he muttered.

The crowd whooped and clapped, and a voice yelled: "His mom will be *so* proud!" and suddenly Doreen Heckle-Flipper pushed herself forward. "Hi, I'm Jackson's mom's best friend," she said, waving at the camera. "Marina had to go home because she was sick, but she'll be watching at home, and she'll be bursting with pride. Hi, Marina!" she said, peering into the camera. "We're all looking after Jackson and your Egg for you, so don't you worry about a thing, honey."

"That's great to hear," Bill Feathers said. "And tell us, Jackson, where do you get your amazing skills from?"

Jackson shrugged. "Um—err—" He wanted

to explain that they were secret agent techniques, that he and Quigley practiced for hours, but there was NO WAY he could do that on camera. Not now that he knew his mom was probably watching.

"Oh, Jackson's always been very active," Doreen Heckle-Flipper answered for him. "I remember him walking along my fence when he was a hatchling, dressed up in frilly pants like a sweet little acrobatic clown!"

There were a few chuckles from the crowd and some "So cute!" comments. Jackson glanced at Quigley. *Uh-oh.* This interview had the potential for maxing out ten on the wet-your-pants-with-embarrassment scale.

Bill Feathers grinned. "I guess you've known Jackson a long time, then?"

"Oh yes." Doreen beamed. "I've known him since he was an egg, back when he was known as Sweet-Beak!"

What? Jackson felt his cheeks burn. *Nooooooo!* He had to stop her. "Um—yeah, well that was a long time ago," he muttered. "I'm just Jackson now."

Behind the camera, Hoff Rockface was grinning back at him, mouthing the words *Sweet-Beak*. Jackson groaned. How was he ever going to live this down?

"Well, good luck with the next round, Jackson," Bill Feathers said. "And now let's have a few words with Head Judge Wendy Webbingham. So, Wendy, how is the competition going so far?" As the camera turned away, Jackson grabbed Quigley and they slunk off into the crowds.

"Did you hear that?" Jackson groaned. "Mrs. Heckle-Flipper has to be *the* most embarrassing penguin on the planet. I mean, why did she have to say all that stuff about—"

"Listen!" Quigley interrupted. He pointed to his backpack.

"The FBI radio transmitter!" Jackson said. "Maybe they've caught Icejob!"

They huddled behind a snack wagon with the transmitter up close to their ears.

Calling all agents, calling all agents. There's been a sighting of escaped criminal Icejob outside Rookeryville Museum at the Golden Egg Games arena. All agents respond!

"Flapping frost feathers!" Jackson gasped. "Icejob's here!"

Jackson glanced around, peering at the faces of the spectator penguins. "If Icejob's in disguise, he could be any one of them," he whispered to Quigley. "He could be that teenager over there. Or that kid with the balloon. Or that mom penguin. Or even—Victor!"

They stared across at Victor, the smiley penguin who owned Brain Freezers, their favorite snack shack. Victor's place was where they planned most of their secret missions. But today Victor was out of his café and serving ice cream from his mobile cart. He waved when he saw them looking at him.

"Nah, not Victor," Quigley said, waving back. "He could never be fake."

Jackson shrugged. "Whoever Icejob is pretending to be, he's obviously about to sneak in and steal that jewel. We've got to stop him. If only we could leave the Games and go stake out the museum."

"I could go," Quigley suggested.

Jackson sighed. "Yeah, I guess that's a good plan."

"I'll keep in touch via walkie-talkie," Quigley said. "Hey—there's Lily. I think she's looking for you."

"Jackson!" Lily came running over. "They've started the next round, and Hoff's boasting about how he's going to win."

Jackson rolled his eyes. "Okay, I'm coming." He picked up the Egg and followed Lily through the crowds.

"Hey, where did Quigley go?" Lily asked.

"Um . . . he just had something he had to do. So, can you explain what this challenge is exactly?"

"It's the Egg-streme Aerial Adventure," Lily said. "You've got to carry your egg up that tall tower." She pointed to a high wooden plat-form. "Then cross a tightrope to the platform on the other side and rappel down."

"And that's it?" Jackson asked.

"Only the five fastest penguins go through to the final," Lily said. "Uh-oh—look at the leaderboard. Hoff's already completed the challenge."

Jackson groaned. "And set a new course record!" He had a sudden vision of spending the next seven days scrubbing the mud off Hoff's filthy flipper-ball boots. He gritted his beak. No way was he going to let Hoff win. "Where do I have to go?"

"Over there." Lily pointed to the line of competitors waiting to take their turn. "I'll meet you at the other end. Good luck."

He shuffled over, laying the Egg down by his feet. He checked out the competition. There were a couple of teenagers, a penguin wearing a DADS ROCK T-shirt, and two penguins Jackson recognized from the Mom Squad. "Well, at least Mrs. Heckle-Flipper's not here," he whispered to the Egg. He glanced down. *Huh? Where did it go?* A wave of panic swept through his feathers. "Egg?" he called.

"Excuse me," an old wobbly voice from behind said. "Is this yours?"

Jackson turned to find a grandma penguin
with thick makeup and a flowery head scarf.

"Oh thanks," Jackson said, taking his soon-
to-be-sibling from her. "Naughty Egg!" he said
in a stern voice. "You shouldn't roll off like
that." He glanced back at the grandma penguin. "Thanks so much."

"Oh, no problem." The grandma penguin
bent down and pulled her own small egg out

of her bag. "I'm hoping this one doesn't hatch while I'm climbing that rope!"

Jackson blinked at her. "*You're* competing in the Games?" He felt his face grow hot. "I mean, it's great that you're competing—"

"Sure!" the grandma penguin interrupted. "I'm a strong old bird." And she flexed one of her muscled flippers.

Whoa, Jackson thought. *Her muscles are almost as big as Mom's.*

"Next in line, please!" A tall penguin wearing a helper T-shirt gestured to Jackson to step forward. "We're just waiting for one of the previous competitors to return their safety harness," she said. "Oh look, here's one coming now. Thanks, young man."

Hoff was shoving his way past another competitor, rushing to hand his harness to Jackson. "Good luck, *Sweet-Beak*," he said

with a smirk, then under his breath he added,
"You're gonna need it!"

"What do you mean?" Jackson called as
Hoff slunk away.

"Please step into the harness," the organizer
penguin said, "and I'll fasten it up."

Jackson did as he was told. But he was
still trying to work out what Hoff had meant
about him needing good luck.

"Okay, it's nice and secure," the organizer
penguin said, giving the harness a tug. "Now,
when I blow the whistle, you put your Egg in
your backpack, then go and pull yourself up
the side of this tower using the rope. Don't
worry if you fall," she added, "your harness
will save you."

Jackson tugged at the straps. It felt okay,
but—

"When you get to the platform at the top,"
she went on, "your Egg must roll itself across

the plank to the other side while you walk the tightrope, then you both rappel down. Are you ready?" She put her whistle in her beak.

"Yeah, I guess," Jackson said. "But maybe we should check the harness one more—"

Too late! The organizer penguin had already blown her whistle.

"**I** 've got a bad feeling about this," Jackson muttered to the Egg as he shoved it into his backpack and reached for the seaweed rope that was dangling down the side of the tower. He took a deep breath. "Okay, let's do this!" And he began pulling himself up, flipper over flipper.

"Ughhhh," he groaned. His backpack hadn't felt heavy when he'd set off, but now— *It feels like Hoff and all his buddies sneaked inside.* Jackson glanced down at the ground. He really hoped Hoff hadn't messed with the harness.

If it snaps, he thought, *we'll both be scrambled.*

Jackson was halfway up when he felt it: an itch on his belly. He wriggled, wishing he had a free flipper to scratch with. *Come on, 00Zero*, he told himself. *This is not hard! You climb a rope to bed every night!* Jackson's dad had recently built him a super-high high-sleeper bed shaped like a nest perched on a rocky cliff, with a long rope to climb to get into it. Jackson's dad loved remodeling their home, and his latest fad was extreme rooms. Jackson's sister, Finola, now had a water room with a floating bed boat!

Urgh, what is *that itch?* Jackson squirmed and jiggled. *Maybe this is part of the challenge,* he thought. *Maybe the rope's made of some sort of scratchy seaweed.* He grimaced . . . *So itchy . . . Got to scratch!* He screwed up his eyes. *Can't scratch . . . Can't let go of the rope . . .*

Jackson dragged himself up until there

were just a few feet to go. *Keep going, 00Zero, nearly there.* Then—"Made it!" He flopped onto the platform at the top, grabbing at his belly and scratching like a baboon. "Huh?" He watched as tiny little insects ran up his flippers. "Urgh! Itchy ice ants!" The harness was crawling with them. Jackson let out a growl. "Hoff Rockface! I know it was you!" Then he remembered what he'd said when Hoff had been taunting him before the contest started. And how he'd told Hoff he could win even if he was covered in slippy seaberry juice and itchy ice ants! *Grrrr!* Jackson clenched his flippers.

"Are you okay over there?" An organizer penguin on the platform at the other side of the tightrope was waving to him. "Do you need first aid?"

Jackson jumped up. "Nah, I'm fine, thanks." He flicked off as many ants as he could. "There's only one way out of this," he muttered, pulling the Egg out of the backpack. "To get down as fast as possible!"

Jackson laid the Egg on the long plank that stretched across to the other platform. "Okay, so you roll, I walk. And p-l-e-a-s-e be fast!" Jackson had one final scratch, then grabbed the guide rope above him and set off across the tightrope. "Whoa," he muttered as a sudden blast of icy wind buffeted him. He shivered. *I hope that storm Mom was talking about isn't about to blow in now. No way do I want to be tightrope walking up here in a blizzard! And what about the Egg! How would it*

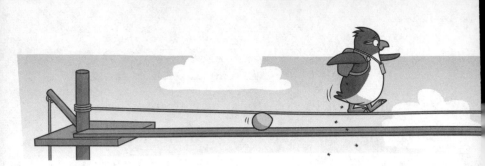

cope in a freezing storm? He didn't dare look at it. What if it wasn't even rolling alongside him?

"Wow, Jackson!" he heard Lily shout from below. "You guys are like a couple of tornadoes!"

"We are?" Jackson glanced sideways. *Wow! The Egg is rolling! Yes!*

Head down, beak clenched, Jackson zipped across the rope and made it onto the other platform. A heartbeat later, the Egg joined him.

"Coming through!" Jackson yelled to the organizer penguin as he scooped up the Egg bowling-ball-style and sped past her. Jackson gripped another seaweed rope, with the Egg under one flipper, and began rappelling down. Half a dozen giant hops later, he clattered onto the ground, panting and puffing and ripping off the itchy harness.

"Well done!" said a Games official, peering at her stopwatch. "That was fast."

But Jackson was more interested in getting rid of the ants. "Urgh! They're everywhere!" He ran his flipper through his crest and shook out his tail.

"You did it!" Lily came running over, beaming at him. "You're second on the leaderboard. Look, just behind Hoff. You could still beat him in the next round."

Jackson grinned. "Hey, little guy," he said, tickling the Egg. "We did it!"

"Good work, Jackson." Doreen Heckle-Flipper and a couple other penguins from the Mom Squad came shuffling over. "I think we're soon gonna have to start calling you Mayor Rockflopper!"

The Games official next to them shook her head. "Don't count your chicks. Look up there!"

The head scarf–wearing grandma penguin who'd been behind Jackson in the line bounded across the tightrope above them, almost in one leap.

"Is she flying?" Jackson muttered, his eyes wide like saucers.

"Hey, Jackson," Lily said. "I just heard a tapping sound—from your Egg. When is it due to hatch?"

"Hopefully not today," Jackson said, checking the shell for cracks. *I've got enough on my flippers with games and jewels and catching escaped criminals.* "Maybe you should get some sleep now," he told the Egg, sliding it back inside his backpack. As he did, he spotted his walkie-talkie. *Quigley!* He had to check in with his buddy.

"I was thinking, Jackson," Mrs. Heckle-Flipper said, "there's a break for lunch now, so I could help you prepare for the final round with some Zumba-Flipper warm-up exercises. See, like this—"

Jackson watched goggle-eyed as Mrs. Heckle-Flipper stretched out her flippers and started leg bending. "Um—thanks," he said, backing away. "Only I kind of need the bathroom. Back soon." He waved to Lily, then shuffled off, checking over his shoulder to make sure none of them were following him. He slipped behind a balloon stand and clicked the talk button on his walkie-talkie. "This is 00Zero calling Agent Q," he whispered. "Come in, Agent Q." For a few moments nothing happened. Then—

"This is Agent Q, calling Agent 00Zero," Quigley responded. "There have been major developments."

Jackson felt a ripple of excitement through his feathers. "Have you seen the suspect?"

"No, but I just found a toolbox in the museum cloakroom and guess what is inside" —the walkie-talkie crackled—"a prison uniform!"

Jackson gasped. "That means Icejob *must*

be there. Stand by. I'm on my way."

But before Jackson could move, an alarm began to sound, and moments later, the museum doors crashed open and visitor penguins began to pour out.

"WOULD ALL PENGUINS PLEASE REMAIN EXACTLY WHERE THEY ARE?!" shouted an FBI agent with a megaphone. "THERE IS NO FIRE. REPEAT: THERE IS NO FIRE!"

"What's going on?" Jackson sidled up to a group of young Flipper Scouts and their leader, who were chatting excitedly outside the museum.

"There's been a robbery," a penguin with a green bow in her crest said. "Someone stole a rare sapphire!"

Jackson groaned. *So Icejob had done it! He'd stolen the Ice Dragon's Eye.*

"We thought it was a fire," the little penguin added. "The alarm went off, so we all rushed outside."

So did everyone else, Jackson thought, looking around at the hundreds of penguins who had poured out of the museum. *Which means Icejob would have been able to escape the scene of his crime by mixing in with all the visitors evacuating the museum. Clever!*

"*NO ONE MUST LEAVE THE AREA!*" the FBI agent with the megaphone shouted. "*STAY EXACTLY WHERE YOU ARE!*"

Other agents were moving around the groups of penguins now, taking statements. Jackson waited until their backs were turned, then he darted up the steps and slipped through the museum doors.

"Jackson!" Quigley grabbed his buddy's

flipper and tugged him behind a pillar. "How did you get inside? The museum's on lockdown."

"The FBI is in a bit of a flap," Jackson whispered. "They're not paying as much attention as you'd expect."

Quigley nodded. "Can you believe it? Icejob actually managed to steal the jewel when the FBI was guarding it."

Jackson nodded. "Even Uncle Bryn couldn't stop it from happening. We should go find him."

"Sure, I know a shortcut to the jewel room. Follow me."

Quigley led Jackson through the crowds of penguins huddled in the museum entrance hall, down a corridor, and along to a back staircase.

"One more floor to go," Quigley panted as they reached the second level. "Hey, how did you escape the Games? You didn't lose, did you?"

"Nah, they're having a break for lunch. But I'm not going back. No way can the FBI crack this case alone."

They'd reached the third floor landing, and Quigley led Jackson through a doorway onto a bright corridor lined with exhibits: chunky rocks, unusual crystals, and a huge meteor that sparkled under the lights.

"The jewel room is just down there," Quigley whispered. "But I should warn you, the FBI boss wasn't too friendly when I popped my head in earlier."

"*Stop right there!*" boomed a voice, and Senior Agent Frost-Flipper thundered down the corridor with a fierce expression on her beak. "What in the name of Neptune are you two doing here?" She glared at Quigley. "I told *you* to go away earlier—and now *you're* here, too!" She scowled at Jackson, her beady eyes boring into his.

"We're here to help," Jackson said, his voice sounding strangely squeaky under her red-hot gaze. "W-w-we heard about the stolen jewel. And we're going to find it for you."

"*You're* going to find it?" Senior Agent Frost-Flipper snorted. "If the entire FBI couldn't stop it from being stolen, what makes you think you're going to be able to find it?"

Jackson was about to explain that he and Quigley had already solved two FBI cases, when there was a shout and an agent poked his head out of a door. "We've found something among the broken glass, boss."

Senior Agent Frost-Flipper shuffled back down the hall. "What is it?"

Jackson nodded to Quigley that they should follow her.

"This," the agent said, holding up a small card.

Jackson leaned forward and read:

Senior Agent Frost-Flipper let out a growl. "Icejob!" She clenched her flippers tightly. "He's laughing at us!"

Jackson coughed. "Um—according to the *Secret Agent Handbook*, Chapter 6, Section 3, when criminals stop taking their crimes seriously, they're usually close to making a mistake."

"Thank you, Jackson!" Senior Agent Frost-Flipper said. "I wrote that book, so I don't need you to repeat it."

"You wrote it?" Jackson's beak fell open. He glanced at Quigley, then back at her. "Oh, my—I mean—wow!"

The FBI boss rolled her eyes and stalked into the jewel room, closely followed by Jackson and Quigley.

The room was small and made smaller by the number of secret agents squashed inside. Some were dusting for flipperprints. Others were taking pictures. A few were huddled in the corner, talking in low voices. Uncle Bryn was one of them.

"That's where the Ice Dragon's Eye was kept," Quigley whispered, pointing to an

empty plinth in the middle of the room surrounded by piles of smashed frost glass.

Jackson stepped over the fragments to read the information panel that was fixed underneath where the glass case had stood. "Wow, that jewel really was the color of ice," he said, peering at a picture of it.

"Hey—have you noticed the windows?" Quigley whispered.

Jackson glanced over, his eyes narrowing. "That's weird. Why would Icejob break all the windows?"

"Maybe that's how he got in?" Quigley suggested.

"Jackson?" Uncle Bryn shuffled across the room. "Be careful of the broken glass."

"Hi, Uncle Bryn," Jackson said. "We came to help."

"Oh, um—that's kind." Uncle Bryn glanced at his boss, who was glaring at them from across the room. "Only, I think you need to go now. This is a crime scene."

"Don't worry, we haven't touched anything," Jackson said.

"Absolutely nothing!" Quigley said, putting his flippers behind his back.

Jackson leaned in closer to his uncle. "So what leads have you got? Did Icejob break in through the windows?"

Uncle Bryn shook his head. "There were six of us in here the whole time. There's no way he could have come in without us seeing him."

"Unless he hypnotized you!" Quigley said.

Uncle Bryn blushed. "Not this time. And besides, we had agents posted outside the door and down the hall."

"What about up there?" Jackson pointed to a hatch in the roof.

"We'd have seen him if he rappelled into

the room." Uncle Bryn sighed. "It's as though he was wearing a cloak of invisibility."

"Oh, wow, like those sardine suits I made!" Quigley nudged his buddy. "Remember?"

Jackson grimaced. How could he forget. "So what are you going to do?" he asked his uncle.

Before Bryn could reply there was the *flip-flap-flip-flap* sound of running footsteps, and an agent burst into the room. "Boss! Boss!" she panted, calling to Senior Agent Frost-Flipper. "There's been another robbery." She caught her breath as all eyes turned toward her. "The Golden Egg Cup has been stolen!"

You could have knocked Jackson over with a feather. *Two robberies in one day!*

Senior Agent Frost-Flipper's face turned ghost-gray. "W-w-what happened?"

The agent shrugged. "The museum alarm went off, and when the judges turned back around, the cup had vanished."

Jackson leaned in close to Quigley. "An opportunist criminal," he whispered. "The thief saw the panic at the museum and used the chaos as a distraction to steal the cup."

Senior Agent Frost-Flipper silenced him

with a scowl. Then she looked around the room. "Okay, this is what we're going to do. Agent Wind-Blower," she said, looking at a penguin with an enormous tail. "You take charge in here. And Agents Rockflopper, Feather-Freckle, and Wing-a-ling," she said, pointing to Uncle Bryn and two of his colleagues. "Follow me. We're going to find out exactly what has happened."

"You know what this means," Jackson whispered to Quigley as they followed the agents down the museum stairs. "Whoever has stolen the cup can put their name on it and become mayor!"

"What? Even if they're a thief?" Quigley shook his head. "That's so unfair."

Jackson nodded. "That's why the cup is kept locked up."

Senior Agent Frost-Flipper spun around. "You two! Go home, now! Or I'll call your moms."

Uncle Bryn coughed. "Well, actually, Jackson's supposed to be taking part in the Golden Egg Games."

"That's true," Jackson squeaked. "Look!" He rummaged in his backpack. "Here's my Egg— Whoa—did you see that?" he added to Quigley. "The shell sort of moved."

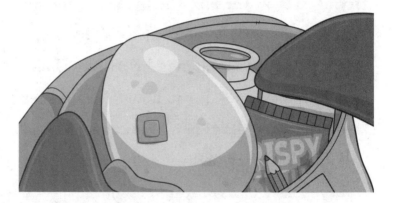

"Yeah," Quigley said. "Like it's trying to fight its way out!"

"Great!" Senior Agent Frost-Flipper snapped. "Then perhaps you should take your egg home. A criminal investigation is no place for a newborn hatchling, or ANY hatchling for that matter." She stomped down the last few steps and through the double doors at the bottom, with Uncle Bryn and the other agents racing after her.

"Now listen, buddy," Jackson said, waggling his flipper at the Egg. "You are not allowed to hatch right now, because we are really busy trying to show the FBI why they need to hire us. So if you stay in your shell today, I'll—" He frowned and scratched his crest. "Um— well, I'll maybe teach you how to be a secret agent someday, okay? Now, how about you go into my backpack and get some sleep. Mom said you need loads of rest." He shoved it back inside and headed down the stairs. "Come on," he called to Quigley. "We've got to catch up to them."

Outside, there was chaos.

Dozens of Games officials were huddled in groups, whispering and pointing. FBI agents were trying to stop spectator penguins from leaving. And Bill Feathers, the TV reporter for *Rookery Live*, was interviewing anyone who would talk to him.

Senior Agent Frost-Flipper began barking orders. "I want a temporary control tent erected there so I can start interviewing witnesses. And make sure this whole area is on lockdown; no one is to leave the site until we've spoken to them. And start a bag search. The thief may still be here."

Jackson glanced at Quigley. "She's right. Whoever stole the cup probably hasn't had a chance to escape yet. We should take a look around and see who has a bulky purse or a giant picnic basket." He dropped his backpack on the ground and peered inside. "I've got my bin-ice-ulars in here somewhere."

"I was thinking," Quigley said, peering at the huddles of penguins around them. "The

thief has got to be someone who wants to be mayor, right?"

"Uh-huh," Jackson said, scanning the area through his glasses.

"So it's probably not someone who is still competing," Quigley said. "Because they could still become mayor by winning the contest, right?" He glanced across at the bench where the last remaining contestants were waiting. "So we're looking for someone who didn't make it through to the third round—a sore loser."

Before Jackson could reply, the FBI agent with the megaphone climbed up onto a box. "We are about to carry out a bag inspection. Thank you for your cooperation!"

"Come on," Jackson said. "There's Uncle Bryn. Let's go ask him if he's got any new leads." He picked up his backpack and went to put his bin-ice-ulars inside, when— "The Egg!" he gasped. "It's gone."

Jackson started frantically checking under bushes. "This disaster is in a whole new dimension of disasters!" Jackson said. "If we don't find the Egg, Mom is going to go off the Shark Scale of Crossness and onto a whole new scale of prehistoric mega-sharks. Think T. rex crossed with Great White, then add some tusks and—"

"I've just thought of something," Quigley interrupted.

"This isn't the time for thinking," Jackson said. "Let's go ask Victor if he's seen it."

But Quigley was staring at his watch. "Victor won't have seen the Egg," he said, turning to look in the other direction, "because according to my tracker patch app, which you'll remember I stuck on its shell, the Egg is right over—there!" He pointed to the competitors' bench.

Jackson followed Quigley's pointing finger. There were five contestants, counting him, still left in the contest. And the four others—including Hoff Rockface—were sitting on the bench, waiting for the Games to restart.

"Come on," Quigley said. "Let's check."

"Hoi, *Sweet-Beak*!" Hoff Rockface growled. "Why are you looking in my backpack?"

"I'm not," Jackson said. "I'm just checking behind it for—"

"Wait a minute." Hoff's eyes narrowed. "Are you accusing me of stealing that cup? Because if you are—"

"There it is!" Quigley shouted from farther down the line. "Next to that lady's purse."

Jackson looked where Quigley was looking. *Huh? Oh no, not again!* He raced down the line to retrieve the Egg from behind the feet of the same grandma penguin it had been bothering earlier.

"Oh!" she gasped, grabbing her bags close to her, as though she thought Jackson was coming to take them.

"No, no, it's just my Egg," Jackson said, scooping up his soon-to-be-sibling. "I don't know why it keeps rolling over to you." He sniffed the air. Something smelled familiar. "Um—maybe it's your perfume. I think it smells a lot like the stuff our Granny Rockflopper uses."

"Don't worry," the grandma penguin said, standing up. "I'm just about to go home, so perhaps that'll help."

"Aren't you staying for the rest of the Games?" Jackson asked, slipping the Egg into his backpack.

"No, I'm too tired." The grandma penguin yawned, and Jackson noticed how thick her makeup was. *Even thicker than Finola's, and she takes at least three hours to paste hers on.* Jackson knew exactly how long that took, because every morning he was left hopping around the landing, waiting to use the bathroom.

The grandma penguin sighed. "There's so much waiting around, and I'm exhausted."

Jackson wasn't surprised; the grandma penguin had flown around the course like a rocket-propelled pigeon!

Just then, there was a shout.

"Competitor penguins, please may I have your attention!" Wendy Webbingham had appeared, along with a group of helper penguins—including Lily. Behind them, Jackson could see Bill Feathers, the TV reporter, and his camera-penguin.

"Everyone huddle around, please," Wendy Webbingham called.

Jackson and the grandma penguin left their bags by the bench and joined the other competitors in front of the judge.

"Congratulations on having reached the final round of the competition," Wendy Webbingham said. "Unfortunately, due to the theft of the cup, we've decided to stop the Games."

There were gasps and groans and shouts of "No way!"

Jackson noticed Bill Feathers, the TV reporter, moving in closer. His camera-penguin had her lens pointed at the unhappy competitors.

Hoff's flipper shot up in the air. "But shouldn't the penguin at the top of the leaderboard just be declared the winner?" He puffed out his feathers. "Because that would be me."

Jackson held his breath. *Please no!*

Wendy Webbingham shook her head. "The final round is the most important one.

It involves showing special egg-caring skills. Without winning the final round, it's impossible to prove you've got *all* the skills a mayor should have."

Hoff snorted. "It looks like the only skill you need is thieving flippers!"

Wendy Webbingham gave him a hard stare. "If the cup is found before the end of the day, the contest will resume. Otherwise, the next Games will be held in ten years' time."

The group erupted in groans and moans.

"Pardon me," said the grandma penguin, her voice sounding older and wobblier than before. "I'm afraid I've decided to withdraw. I'm just too tired to wait around. Please could you escort me to the museum so I can call a taxi? I must admit I find all these FBI agents quite alarming."

"Of course, ma'am!" Wendy Webbingham held out her flipper. "Let me help you—oh, yes, you go get your bags first—"

Sheesh, Jackson thought, watching them leave. *That grandma penguin really does look exhausted. She's all bent over—nothing like the way she moved earlier.*

"Hi, Jackson," Lily said, coming over. "It's such a shame the contest is on hold. You were doing so well."

"Thanks," Jackson said, but he was still watching the grandma penguin, who was gathering up her belongings while chatting to the judge. *She sure has a lot of bags*, he thought. *It's like Dad when we go for a picnic.*

"Hey, did you see Hoff Rockface?" Quigley asked as he joined them. "He's telling everyone he should be declared winner of the Games, that he's been cheated!"

Lily rolled her eyes. "He's such a sore loser."

"Hey—speaking of sore losers," Jackson said. "Lily, do you know where the book of competitors is? The one they wrote our names in when we registered?"

"Why?" Lily frowned. "This isn't some crazy scheme to join the FBI, is it?"

Jackson felt his face heating up. "No—well, yes, maybe." He grinned. "It's just, we were thinking. The person who stole the cup is probably someone who lost in the earlier rounds. Like Quigley said, a sore loser."

"Yeah, I guess that's a possibility," Lily said. "And you want to see their names so you can investigate them as suspects?" She paused, mulling the idea over. "I don't know, Jackson.

That book is stored in the museum office, and only official Games' helpers are allowed in there."

Jackson made a pleading face. "Please, Lily. If we can find the suspect, we might find the trophy."

"Which means the Games can restart," Quigley said. "And Jackson might beat Hoff!"

Lily looked across at Hoff, who was now moaning on camera to Bill Feathers, the TV reporter. "Okay," she said. "I guess a little peek wouldn't hurt. Come on, I'll show you where it is."

But as Jackson went to grab his backpack, he heard someone calling his name.

"Jackson! Jackson Rockflopper! Has anyone seen a young man called— Oh, there he is! Jackson, I've been looking *everywhere* for you."

If Jackson could have squeezed himself under the competitors' bench to hide, he would have done so. "Oh, hi, Mrs. Heckle-Flipper," he mumbled. Behind her he could see Lily and Quigley waving to him to hurry up.

"Isn't this missing-cup business dreadful?" Mrs. Heckle-Flipper said. "Especially after that gemstone got stolen." She shook her head. "I can't help thinking that if your mom was here, none of this would have happened."

Jackson nodded. No one would *dare* try to

steal anything under Marina Rockflopper's beak. She had the best arrest record in the history of Waddles', the department store where she worked.

"Oh, by the way, I called your mom," Mrs. Heckle-Flipper said. "And I offered to drop you boys home."

"B-b-but the contest isn't over yet," Jackson said, a sudden panic passing through his feathers. "If they find the cup, the competition is going to restart."

Mrs. Heckle-Flipper sighed. "I don't think that's likely. Whoever took the cup is probably long gone. Wait—let me check the time on my cell."

While she rummaged in her purse, Jackson glanced over at Quigley and Lily. *HELP!* he mouthed.

"Well, perhaps we can give it another hour," Mrs. Heckle-Flipper said, peering at the screen of her icePhone. "The FBI agent who checked my bag said they would be taking statements from anyone who saw anything. And as I told him, I've probably got lots of useful information to pass along."

She babbled on and on, but Jackson was distracted by Quigley and Lily, who were now talking to Victor by his ice cream cart. *What are they doing?* Now was not the time for snacking!

"Oh look!" Mrs. Heckle-Flipper said, waving to the other moms across the arena. "Over here!" she called to them. "I found Jackson!"

What? Noooooo! Jackson groaned. Mrs. Heckle-Flipper was bad enough, but if the whole group was going to be "eyes on," he'd never escape.

As the other moms shuffled over, Victor appeared, too. "Free ice cream!" he called, trundling his cart up to the group.

Huh? Jackson glanced across at Quigley and Lily, who were grinning and giving him a flippers-up.

"Free?" Mrs. Heckle-Flipper said. "How come?"

"Because you're my one hundredth customer of the day!" Victor winked at Jackson. "It's a Brain Freezers special promotion. And you and your friends all get a free ice cream. Ooh, you've got to check out my new flavor, Rookeryville Road. It's real fancy! Or how about Blizzard Brownie?" He glanced up at the darkening sky. "Just the right flavor with a storm brewing!"

As the moms crowded around to look in the cart, Jackson backed away. "I'll just fetch Quigley," he murmured. "I don't want him to miss out." Then he raced off before they could stop him. "How did you do that?" he whispered to Quigley as soon as they were out of earshot.

"It was Lily's idea," Quigley said. "She told Victor that your mom's buddies had shared their picnic snacks with us, and we wanted to repay their kindness, but that they wouldn't let us treat them."

"So I asked Victor to be creative in handing out the ice cream," Lily said.

"Awesome escape plan!" Jackson smiled at her.

Lily's face turned shrimp pink. "Oh, well, Quigley paid for the ice cream."

"I used the money your mom gave us," Quigley said. "Hope that's okay."

"Sure!" Jackson said.

"Here, put these on," Lily said. "Two of the volunteers had to go home, so I borrowed their T-shirts. It's just in case we get stopped on the way to the office."

"Ha! Check this out," Quigley said, pointing at the words on the front of his shirt. "I'm EGG-cited to help!"

"Now I know how Icejob feels," Jackson said, tugging his down. "With this disguise, I

actually feel like I'm a real volunteer. Maybe I should go help a few people on the way."

"Don't do that!" Lily gasped. "The other volunteers might spot that you guys are fake— hey, I think that FBI agent is waving you over."

"Hi!" the agent called. "I need to check your bags before you can leave this area— Oh, pardon me," she said, peering at their shirts. "I didn't see you were helpers. You can go straight through."

Lily led the way back into the museum. "The office is just off this hall," she whispered. "Hopefully there won't be anyone in— Oh, hi, Miah." Lily smiled at another young volunteer, who was coming the other way. "I'm just going to fetch some—um—balloons! Come on, guys."

Jackson thought the office looked a lot like his bedroom: stuffed full of useful stuff! As well as boxes of balloons, there were piles of leaflets, dozens of T-shirts, along with bags of badges and other promotional gifts. And on the wall, a large map of the layout of the Golden Games courses, with pins and flags stuck in it.

"Wow, they really thought this out," Quigley said, peering at the map.

"Well, they did have ten years to plan it," Jackson pointed out.

"Quick, you guys," Lily whispered. "The book is on the desk over there. You look while I guard the door. Hurry!"

Jackson began turning the pages. "Oh, wow, look—it goes back decades. Sheesh! These old-fashioned names are so cool."

"Willoughby Bark-Wobble," Quigley read. "Lettuce Flutter-Wick. Marta Muddle-Feather."

"Guys!" Lily said.

Jackson flicked through the pages a little faster. "Hey," he said. "Check this out . . .

Marina Silverfish! That's my mom!"

"Huh?" Quigley cocked his head to one side. "Marina Silverfish?"

"That was her name before she married my dad. Look," Jackson said, "she entered the Games twenty years ago. She must have been our age back then. Wow, I never knew she'd competed."

Quigley peered at the page. "Yeah, it says she took part with her soon-to-be-sibling."

"That must have been my Aunt Astrid," Jackson said.

"I wonder how far they got in the contest," Quigley said, scanning down to the bottom of the page. "Maybe it will tell us."

But Jackson wasn't looking at his mom's name now. He was staring at the one below it. "Flying Flippers!" he breathed. "I don't believe it!"

"**C**ustard **Dorkfin?" Quigley read. "But** that's Icejob's name."

Jackson nodded. "Which means he must have entered the same year my mom did."

"And lost," Quigley said. "See there—the winner's name is at the bottom of the page, and it isn't Custard Dorkfin."

"Custard Dorkfin?" Lily frowned. "That's weird. He's in the contest today, too."

"He can't be," Jackson said. "Custard Dorkfin is the real name of a criminal called Icejob. He broke out of jail this morning, and the FBI thinks he stole the Ice Dragon's Eye."

"He's definitely in today's contest." Lily stepped over to the table and flicked through to the front of the book. "See, there it is. I was at the registration desk first thing this morning. And when I looked through the book, I thought it was strange that this name didn't have an address next to it."

Jackson scratched his crest. "But I don't understand. Why would Icejob have entered the Golden Games?"

"Perhaps he was upset that he didn't win last time he took part," Lily suggested. "Maybe he's a sore loser."

"Or maybe it's not him. Maybe there are just two penguins called Custard Dorkfin," Quigley said. "I think there's another penguin in the second grade called Jackson."

"Yeah, and two Lilys in the first grade," Lily added.

Jackson puffed out his cheeks. "Do you really think two sets of parents would be crazy enough to call their kid Custard Dorkfin?" He sighed. "But if it is Icejob, someone would have spotted him. There were FBI agents everywhere. And he's got this really distinctive ice-crystal tattoo on his beak."

"Don't forget he's a master of disguise," Quigley said.

"And he could have been wearing make-up," Lily suggested. "My auntie works at the theater, and she makes the actors look really different: fake beaks, false feathers. She even gives them pretend zits and scars. Everything!"

Jackson stared at the name in the book; an idea was gnawing at his brain. "So if Icejob was competing in the Games, in disguise, maybe he stole both the jewel *and* the trophy?"

"Impossible!" Quigley said. "He couldn't be in two places at the same time, unless"—his eyes widened—"he's invented a time-travel machine."

Jackson smiled. "I don't think the guards in the jail would have let him do anything like that."

"Yeah, and plus it's really hard," Quigley said. "Me and Sunny tried it once. Sunny put his pet goldfish in it and we haven't seen it since."

Lily grimaced. "Remind me *never* to help with your experiments."

Jackson scanned the names of the other competitors, then he closed the book. "It's just too much of a coincidence. It's got to be Icejob. He must have stolen both the sapphire and the trophy. Somehow we need to figure out how he could be in two places at the same time."

"Shush!" Lily said. "Someone's coming." She pushed the book back to where it had been in the middle of the desk, then— "Here, hold these—" she said, handing them some balloons. "Oh, hi, Mrs. Webbingham," Lily said as the door opened. "We're just getting some toys for the little hatchlings to play with while they wait for the Games to restart."

"Oh, what a good idea," Wendy Webbingham said. "Everyone is getting so restless." She looked at Jackson and then Quigley, and then back to Jackson again. "You look familiar."

"This is Jackson and Quigley," Lily said. "Jackson's in the contest; he did really well in round one."

"Of course!" Wendy Webbingham said. "Such a unique ice-sliding style."

"Jackson and Quigley have offered to help me entertain the hatchlings," Lily said, "until the Games start up again."

"Oh, that's so kind!" Wendy Webbingham

said. "Hopefully the missing trophy is just a prank and it'll be returned soon. Meanwhile, the FBI has asked to see this." She picked up the competitors' book from the table. "I'd better get it over to them." And she shuffled out of the office, closing the door behind her.

"We'd better go, too," Lily said.

As they headed back into the main hall, Quigley nudged Jackson. "Look, there's Sunny— Hi, Sunny!"

His older cousin was carrying a large laptop. He waved when he saw them. "Hey, cuz—I like the shirts. I didn't know you dudes were helping with the Games. Oh, maybe you can answer a question for me . . ."

"Sure thing." Quigley handed the bag of balloons he'd been carrying to Lily, and shuffled off to talk to his cousin.

"So I guess the FBI will be onto Icejob once they see his name written in that book," Lily said.

Jackson nodded. "Maybe, but I still don't see how he could be in two places at one time. And if he was in the contest, how did he get an egg to compete with? I mean, he's been in jail."

"Maybe he borrowed one," Lily suggested. "It could be his little cousin, or a niece- or nephew-to-be."

"Jackson!" Quigley shouted, waving him over. "You've got to hear this!"

"And I'd better get these outside," Lily said, taking the balloons from Jackson. "Bye for now."

"Jackson!" Quigley was hopping from foot to foot now. "Quick!"

"Okay, okay, keep your feathers on! Hi, Sunny," Jackson said, shuffling over.

"Yo, cuz's friend," Sunny said. Despite the fact that Jackson and Quigley had been buddies since they were eggs, Sunny never remembered Jackson's name.

"Guess what?" Quigley said, his eyes wide as dinner plates. "Sunny was just asking me how the competitor with the 'remote-control egg' was doing in the Games."

"Huh?" Jackson's eyes boggled.

"Yeah, someone actually ordered a remote-control egg from Sunny's new webbed-site," Quigley explained. "Because they didn't have an egg of their own to compete with."

Jackson felt his feathers bristle. "Icejob!" he hissed. "It must have been him! Wait— Sunny, can you check who ordered it?"

"Sure." Sunny flipped open the laptop and began tapping on the keys.

Jackson's eyes were glued to the screen, willing Icejob's name to appear.

"Such a cool site," Quigley said as the title "SunnyScience-ice.com" flitted across the screen, then melted away to reveal the homepage.

Sunny tapped a few more keys, then— "That's weird," he said, scratching his crest.

"The dude who ordered it was in jail. See, it was a Mr. C. Dorkfin of Rookeryville Jail."

"Icejob!" Jackson growled. "I knew it!"

"Whoa!" Sunny's eyes bulged. "That dude ordered loads of stuff." He scrolled down the page. "Mega-Power Wire and Bolt Cutters, solar-powered welding torch, smoke detector, sledgehammer . . ." He chuckled. "Anyone would think he was planning to break out of jail."

Jackson glanced at Quigley. Yet again, Sunny seemed to have been accidentally helping a major criminal mastermind with his crimes.

"Oh neat!" Sunny said. "He ordered one of my new demolition whistles, too. I knew they were going to be big."

"Um—is that the same demolition whistle my dad bought?" Jackson asked. "The one that uses high-frequency sound waves to smash ice? Dad's demolishing our old garage next week," he added to Quigley.

Sunny grinned. "Yep! Your dad loves a gadget. He's one of my best customers. Tell him I've added a new remote-control function to it so that you can demolish anything and you don't have to be anywhere near it. Because safety is always my top consideration when I'm inventing stuff. Right, dudes?"

Jackson snorted. Safety was the *last* thing Sunny's inventions involved. Then suddenly, he froze. "Wait a minute—" His adventure detectors were pulsating now like Christmas lights. "Did you say *remote-control* demolition whistle?"

Sunny nodded. "Yeah, my new demolition whistles now have a distance of two miles. You just put the whistle next to the structure you want to demolish, then you take the remote control and toddle off anywhere you want with it, then *boom*!" He made an explosion motion with his flippers. "Cool, huh!— Wait—that prisoner dude didn't use it to break out of jail, did he?" Sunny gulped. "That might not be cool."

Jackson grabbed Quigley's flipper. "That's it! That's how Icejob was in two places at once!"

"Yeah, I get it!" Quigley said. "He used the remote-control high-frequency demolition whistle to bust the sapphire's ice-glass case!"

"And that's why all the windows were broken, too! Quick," Jackson said, "we've got to get upstairs to the sapphire room. The whistle may still be there. If we find it, we can prove that's how he did it. Come on, Agent Q. Let's do this!"

They raced down the hall, dodging visitor penguins and museum staff, up the stairs to the third floor.

"I thought it was too much of a coincidence," Jackson panted, taking the steps two at a time. "When I saw Icejob's name in that book, I knew it had to be him. Two robberies at the same time! Sheesh!"

They zoomed through the doors and down the hallway to the gemstone room.

"It's kind of quiet up here," Jackson whispered. "No FBI agents?"

"They're probably all out searching for the cup," Quigley said, poking his head around the door of the gemstone room. It was empty now, apart from a janitor with a brush and shovel, who looked up as they crept in.

"Careful, boys," he said in a deep voice. "I've picked up most of the glass, but there may be some pieces left."

"No problem," Jackson said. "We're just looking for something."

The janitor nodded and carried on sweeping.

"Where could it be?" Jackson whispered.

"There aren't too many hiding places in here."

"Over there?" Quigley darted behind the curtains. "Nope, nothing on the windowsill."

Jackson sighed. "I guess it would have been too obvious if he'd left it on top of the glass case. The FBI agents guarding the sapphire would have spotted it."

The janitor threw a shovelful of broken glass into his cart and stood up. "Job done. And I'm out of here! See ya, fellas." And he shuffled off, pushing his cart in front of him.

"I just know it's in here somewhere," Jackson said. "But where?"

Quigley didn't reply. He was staring up at the ceiling.

Jackson followed his gaze. "Nah, that's just a smoke detector. My mom puts them up all over our house."

Quigley's eyes narrowed. "Yeah, but remember Sunny said that Icejob ordered a smoke alarm from his webbed-site. And when the jewel was stolen, someone set the fire alarm off and evacuated the museum, so I'm thinking—" He rummaged in his backpack and pulled out a screwdriver. "Can you give me a leg up?"

Jackson cupped his flippers, and Quigley put his foot on them and scrambled up. "Hoi, watch it!" Jackson staggered a little. "Your knee's in my eye!"

"Nearly there—just two more screws— almost done— Gotcha!" Quigley jumped down, the guts of the smoke alarm in his flipper.

"The whistle!" Jackson said. "You were right! But I still don't get it. How could he have come here to collect the sapphire from the broken case without someone seeing him? There were FBI agents everywhere."

Quigley nodded. "I know. It doesn't add up." He bent down to look at the information panel below the smashed case. "That sapphire sure was unusual, such a pale color, almost looks like—glass."

Jackson blinked at his buddy, his brain cogs turning and whirring and— "Wait—that's it!" he gasped. "Agent Q, you're a genius."

"I am?" Quigley smiled.

"The jewel was *never* stolen," Jackson said, hopping from foot to foot. "Icejob just made it look like it was. It was all a big disguise."

"Um—could you rewind a chapter?" Quigley scratched his crest. "Because I don't get how it wasn't stolen. See—it's not there."

Jackson nodded. "But as you just told me, the sapphire looks like glass, right? Or even a piece of *broken* glass! See! All Icejob needed to do was explode the case, and the sapphire would fall into the pile of broken ice glass, and—"

"No one would notice it!" Quigley shouted. "Yeah, it's just like when you want to hide your favorite candy bar. Where do you keep it? In a bag of candy bars!"

"Except that doesn't work," Jackson said. "I tried it and Dad just ate them all."

Quigley shook his head. "Icejob is so smart. He hid the jewel in the broken glass so he could come get it when all the fuss died down."

"And don't forget that calling card he left," Jackson added. "Another genius idea to make it look like he'd actually stolen the gem. He probably just left the card propped up against the glass case when he installed the whistle."

"Or clipped it on to the outside of the smoke alarm," Quigley said. "See there's a tiny spring loader on the casing—he held it up for Jackson to see. "Icejob could have slotted the card into it, and it would have fallen down when the smoke alarm went off." Quigley stared at Jackson. "You know what all this means, don't you?" His eyes sparkled. "The jewel could still be here in the museum—"

"Yep, inside that janitor's cart!" Jackson said, shuffling for the door. "Come on! We'd better find him before he puts the world's rarest sapphire out in the trash."

"I don't see him," Jackson called to Quigley as he raced down the hallway on the floor below. "I checked the old clocks room, the roman pots section, and the area with all that fancy china. He's not in any of them."

"He's not in the costume rooms, either," Quigley said. "But I did see some cool armor."

"Wait," Jackson said. "Didn't the janitor say he was done? Maybe he didn't just mean he'd finished sweeping up the glass. Maybe he meant he was finished for the day? So perhaps there's a room where he stores his cart."

"I saw that place!" Quigley squealed. "It's in the basement. I noticed it when I was snooping around earlier. I'll show you."

They hurtled back down the stairs. At the bottom, a long dark corridor stretched out in front of them. As they ran along it, they passed several store cupboards and a set of double fire doors leading outside.

"Whoa, it's snowing," Quigley said, peering through the glass. "Just like your mom said it would. Wow, it's getting heavy."

"Is this the place?" Jackson called. He'd stopped in front of a door at the end.

"Yeah, there was no one inside when I snooped earlier," Quigley whispered as he joined him.

Jackson took a deep breath and tapped lightly on the door. They waited. Then he tried again. Still no one answered, so Jackson turned the handle. "Hello? Anyone in here?"

He poked his head around the door. "It's too dark to see anything."

"There's a switch to your right," Quigley said. "Here, let me do it."

Jackson blinked in the sudden light, his eyes scanning the room. Half a dozen cleaning carts stood lined up along one wall. Only one had a bulging trash bag. And draped across the handles was a set of brown overalls.

"Good thing he didn't empty his cart before he left." Jackson glanced in the trash bag. "So much glass! And hopefully one extremely rare sapphire."

"The FBI is *sooo* going to hire us now!" Quigley beamed.

But Jackson was still staring inside the trash cart. "Wait—it's not just glass in here." He peered closer. "It looks like someone's belongings are in here, too. See—there's a makeup compact. And a bottle of perfume. And that looks like a flowery head scarf. And—" He gasped. "A remote-control egg!"

"Huh?" Quigley peered over his shoulder.

"It's a remote-control egg! See? It looks exactly like the one on Sunny's webbed-site." Jackson plucked it out of the trash cart and turned it around and around in his flippers. "Just like the one *Icejob* ordered."

"You think this Egg belongs to Icejob?" Quigley scratched his crest. "But why would Icejob leave it here? And what's it got to do with all the other things in there: the makeup, the flowery head scarf, the perfume . . . ?"

Jackson didn't reply. He reached in and pulled out the bottle of perfume. He pressed the squirter.

"Urgh!" Quigley pinched his beak with his flipper. "That's gross!"

"My Egg doesn't think so," Jackson said. "It loves the smell. That was why it kept bothering that grandma penguin at the Games, remember? It's the same scent our own granny Rockflopper uses."

"Wait—you're not saying these are *your* grandma's things?" Quigley's eyes widened. "Because I really don't think—"

"Nope." Jackson's face hardened. "I think this all belongs to one person: that grandma penguin from the competition!"

Quigley gasped. "Surely you don't think she's working with Icejob?"

"I think she *is* Icejob!" Jackson said. "Check out the makeup." He held up the compact so Quigley could see. "This is not the regular kind like Finola uses. Read the label: STAGE MAKEUP MAX-THICKNESS! Remember what Lily said about her auntie using thick makeup in the theater? If Icejob wanted to cover an ice-crystal tattoo on his beak, I reckon this would do it."

Quigley nodded. "Yeah, yeah, that's true . . . and I guess if the grandma penguin *was* Icejob, it would explain why she was so good at climbing. But I still don't get what all these things are doing here?"

Jackson grabbed the janitor's overalls, still draped over the handles of the cart. He checked the photo ID badge on the front. "Does that penguin in the photo look anything like the janitor we saw upstairs?"

TIANA WINGFEATHER
JANITOR

CITY
MUSEUM

Quigley peered at the picture for a few moments. "Well, not exactly. I mean, the janitor we saw definitely didn't have a blue crest, three purple beak piercings, and an eyebrow ring. And to be honest, I don't think the janitor we saw looked much like someone called"—he peered at the name on the badge—"'Tiana Wingfeather'?"

"It was Icejob!" Jackson clenched his flippers, his eyes narrowing. "He came back for the jewel, just like we thought he would. He left the Games in disguise as that grandma penguin. Mrs. Webbingham even helped carry all his bags, which meant Icejob didn't have to go through the FBI bag check at the Games arena."

"Because if he had," Quigley said, his eyes wide, "then the FBI would have found the big Golden Egg Cup, which he'd just stolen!"

"Exactly!" Jackson said. "Once he'd gotten through the bag check at the Games, he came into the museum, headed straight down here so he could change out of his grandma costume, and borrowed the first janitor's overalls he could find. Then he went up to the jewel room and started clearing up the glass and stole that sapphire from right under our beaks."

"So it's not actually in the trash cart at all?" Quigley said.

Jackson shook his head. "I'd bet my flippers that both the gem and Icejob are long gone."

Quigley groaned. "Icejob sure is smart."

"Yep," Jackson said. "He's at least a ten on the Scary Scale of Evil Geniuses! Come on. We'd better take the remote-control egg and all the grandma-disguise things to show the FBI." He bent down to untie the neck of his bag. "Hey—wakey wakey, little Egg," he said, peering inside. "You're going to have to share your bag with some—" He stopped, a sudden terror flashing across his face. "Quigley," he gasped. "The Egg's gone!"

The room swam in front of Jackson's eyes, and he grabbed the cart to steady himself. "I-i-it must have rolled out when the head judge came to talk to us," he stammered. "That's the last time I saw it. I remember I put my backpack down next to the grandma penguin's bags—"

"You mean *Icejob's* bags," Quigley interrupted.

"Yeah, yeah, next to Icejob's bags, and then we both went over to listen to what the judge had to say." Jackson flicked off the tiny beads of sweat that were now trickling down his face. "The Egg must have rolled out when I wasn't looking." He shuddered. "What if it's got itself lost, or squashed, or—" Jackson swallowed a few times to stop himself blubbering, because secret agents *never* blubbered.

Quigley patted his buddy's flipper. "We'll find the Egg. Don't forget, we've got our secret weapon." He pulled out his icePhone and pressed the screen. "According to the tracker app, your egg is—um—" A puzzled expression appeared on his face. "This can't be right. No way could the Egg have rolled that far."

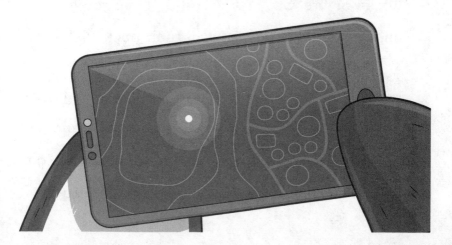

"Where? Let me see." Jackson gulped. "Frostbite Ridge?"

"Nah, something must have gone wrong with the app," Quigley said, tapping the screen. "Eggs don't roll up cliffs. That's against all the laws of physics."

Jackson's feathers were standing on end now, a tidal wave of worry sweeping through them. "M-m-maybe someone kidnapped the Egg!" he said. "And they're escaping with it up Frostbite Ridge."

"Or maybe the tracker patch just fell off." Quigley shrugged. "I mean, that's never happened before, but maybe it did. Then someone picked it up and put it in their pocket."

"Yeah, yeah, that's got to be it," Jackson said, running his flipper through his crest and trying to breathe. "We'll just go back to the bench. The Egg's probably still under there."

But as they went outside, Jackson's head

was swimming with horrible images of what might have happened to the Egg. Lost, stolen, scrambled . . . Suddenly, Icejob and the robberies didn't matter to him anymore. All he could think about was having to tell his mom he'd lost his soon-to-be-sibling. *The Shark Scale of Crossness I can take*, he thought. *But this is* way *beyond that. This will be on a different scale—this will be maxing out on the Scale of Shame*, which was every kid's worst nightmare. Jackson closed his eyes and groaned inside. He was picturing that moment when his mom would tell him she was "disappointed" in him.

"There's Lily!" Quigley said as they ran down the museum steps toward the Games arena. "She'll help us look. Lily! Over here!"

"Hey! Where have you guys been?" Lily wiped the snow out of her eyes and shook her feathers. "We're asking all visitors to take shelter in the museum before the blizzard arrives. Can you help me?"

Jackson shook his head. "Sorry, but I've lost the Egg. I've got to go check the— Hey— they moved the bench!" He looked around desperately. "Where's it gone?"

"They're moving everything inside," Lily explained. "Maybe they found your Egg and put it in the office. Want me to go check?"

"Yes, please," Jackson said.

"Sure, I'll be back in a few minutes." Lily shuffled away, leaving Jackson and Quigley standing in the snow. Nearby, they saw Victor packing up his cart. Next to him were a few groups of FBI agents huddled under umbrellas, still taking statements from visitors. And the Games officials were directing everyone toward the museum for shelter.

"I just don't get it," Quigley muttered, wiping the snow off the screen of his icePhone.

"That tracker app patch had extra-strong glue on it, plus it has an alarm in case it loses contact with its host. I don't see how it could have fallen off the Egg's shell without me realizing."

But Jackson wasn't listening. He was staring at the TV reporter, Bill Feathers, who was interviewing Wendy Webbingham in front of the place where the competitor's bench had been. A tiny bell was ringing in the back of his brain, alerting him to something important. Something to do with Bill Feathers and the Egg, something that could help—"If I could just remember what it is—wait—that's

it! I remember now. Bill Feathers filmed it! He was standing next to us when the head judge came to tell us the competition was being stopped. Maybe he filmed the moment the Egg rolled away, too."

"Huh?" Quigley stopped flicking the snow out of his crest. "Why would he film that?"

"Not intentionally," Jackson explained. "But if the Egg rolled away while he was filming, it might be visible in the background. Come on! We've got to talk to him."

Bill Feathers the TV reporter had finished interviewing the head judge now and was sheltering under a white umbrella, checking his reflection in a hand mirror while his camera penguin fiddled with a box of electrical equipment by his feet.

"Um—pardon me," Jackson said, shuffling over.

Bill Feathers didn't look up. He was prodding his crest with his flipper. "The snow's made my quiff go all floppy," he moaned to himself. "Stupid weather!"

Jackson glanced at Quigley, then coughed. "Um—pardon me, Mr. Feathers."

The TV reporter looked at Jackson, then back at his mirror. "Sorry, I'm a bit too busy to give autographs right now."

"No, no, I don't want your autograph," Jackson began.

"You don't?" Bill Feathers frowned. "Okay, then please go away."

Jackson took a deep breath. "Sir, I need your help with something."

Bill Feathers snapped his mirror shut. "Look, I'm sorry, but we're going live in five, and I've got to prepare, so I don't have time to help with school projects, or to deliver special messages to moms when we're on air— Hey, Rita," he called to the camera-penguin working on the equipment at his feet. "Have you got my comb?"

She looked up, blinking the snow out of her eyes. "It's in the van-sled with your face powder—if you're going to get it, can you bring back a screwdriver?" she added as he shuffled off. "Something's gone seriously wrong with the light and— Suffering squids!" She puffed out her cheeks as the TV reporter disappeared into the crowds without glancing back. "That guy never listens to me!"

"I've got a screwdriver you can borrow," Quigley said, reaching into his backpack. "And, err—I can take a look at your field light, if you like." He leaned over and peered at the large lamp she was working on. "Is that the 745 Starfrost LED Super-Bright, Second-Generation Aluminum X Panel? Because if it is, I think I can fix it."

The camera-penguin blinked more snowflakes out of her eyes. "Huh?"

"My buddy's a bit of a gadget nerd," Jackson explained. "He's got an eidetic memory for instruction manuals."

"An eye-der-down-what?" the camera-penguin said as Quigley blushed and looked at his feet.

"It means he remembers every instruction book he ever looks at," Jackson said. "When he sees one, it's like his brain makes a copy." Jackson held his flippers up to his eyes like he was taking a photograph. "Click! Then that's it. It's in the Quigley memory files forever!"

His buddy's face turned even redder. "Oh, hey, I'm not that good. But—um—I do remember that particular model," he said, pointing to the lamp, "because it had issues with dampness. I guess this snow may have caused it. Can I take a look? I think there's a way to dry it out by blowing on it."

"Sure, kid." The camera-penguin made space for him. "My name's Rita Fettle-Flipper. I'd offer to get you guys an ice cream as a thank-you, but I think Victor's gone home."

Quigley was too busy fiddling with the lamp to reply. But Jackson took his chance.

"There is something else you could do for us," he said, glancing over to make sure Bill Feathers wasn't anywhere nearby. "See, I've lost my Egg. We were competing in the Games together. But I think it may have rolled off while you were filming us earlier."

"Really?" Rita said. "That's bad luck. But how can I help?"

"Well, see, I put my backpack down, over there." Jackson pointed to where the bench had been. "It was when the head judge came over to tell us the competition was being stopped, and that's when the Egg must have rolled out. I remember you were filming, so maybe you caught the moment when it got lost."

She shrugged. "Maybe I did. Let's see." Rita opened a large metal box that contained her camera. She flipped up its viewing screen and pressed a few buttons. "Let me spool back a bit. I guess you heard all about those robberies, yeah?"

Jackson nodded. But he couldn't speak. Images of what might have happened to the Egg were blanking out everything else. *Please be on there*, he thought, staring at the screen and crossing his flippers. If this didn't work, there was only one thing he could do: call his mom. *And I'd rather be covered all over with snappy snow crabs than have to call her!*

"Okay," Rita said, looking at the screen. "So this is the bit when Wendy Webbingham came to tell you all the bad news."

Jackson could see himself and the other competitors lined up in front of the judge. He watched as the camera panned across all their disappointed faces. He peered into the background. "I d-d-don't see it," he whispered, his heart sinking.

"Hold on—I'll rewind and zoom in this time," Rita said.

"Jackson?" Lily came shuffling over. "The Egg's not in the office."

Jackson didn't reply. Somehow he couldn't manage to peel his eyes off the screen. He clenched his flippers, willing the Egg to appear. This time the shot was grainy, the faces of the competitors distorted by the close-up zoom-in. "I don't see—" Jackson began, but then: "—wait—yes! There it is!" he gasped as a tiny white blob in the background moved.

"It's the Egg, and it's rolling and"—Jackson froze—"oh no! I think it rolled into Icejob's backpack!"

"Icejob!" Lily said, peering over his shoulder.

"Icejob?" Rita frowned. "Isn't that the dude they think stole the jewel? Nah, look closer. That backpack belongs to that sweet old grandma. See how she goes and picks it up at the end."

Jackson didn't reply. He just stared at the screen, watching as Icejob, dressed as the grandma, waddled off, leaning on Wendy Webbingham's flipper, carrying the backpack that contained his Egg.

"Hey—I think I've done it," Quigley said. "Stand by for some illumination."

"Whoa—awesome job!" Rita said as they were all suddenly blinded by light.

Jackson blinked in the brightness. The lamp wasn't the only thing suddenly switched on. He felt a sudden surge of energy through his feathers. "Icejob!" he growled under his breath. "You're not going to get away with this. I'm coming for you! Let's do this!"

"So explain that again," Lily said, racing to keep up with Jackson and Quigley as they zoomed across the snow. "You're telling me that the sweet old grandma penguin in the competition was actually Icejob?"

"It was the perfect disguise," Jackson said. "No one ever suspects a sweet old grandma penguin of anything, right?"

Lily nodded. "I guess. And your Egg rolled inside her backpack, which means it's actually inside Icejob's backpack?"

"Yep, you got it," Jackson said, increasing his speed.

"But if the Egg is in Icejob's bag, it could be anywhere!" Lily panted.

"Not exactly," Quigley said. "See, we know where Icejob is, because we put a tracker app patch on the Egg's shell." He smiled. "Neat, huh? At first we couldn't believe the Egg was actually where it was, on account of eggs not being able to roll up cliffs because of gravity."

Lily frowned. "This is getting kind of complicated."

"What Quigley means," Jackson said, "is now that we know the Egg is with Icejob, the location on the tracker app makes sense."

"So where exactly are they?" Lily asked.

Quigley's smile vanished. "Um—halfway up there."

Lily stopped running. She gazed up at Frostbite Ridge, the snow swirling around her head like feathers from a pillow fight. "*No one* would go up there in this weather."

Jackson skidded to a stop. "Well, no one apart from an escaped criminal with a major in ice-climbing, who happens to be on the run with the world's most precious jewel *and* the cup that will make him Mayor of Rookeryville!"

"I guess," Lily said. "But why go up Frostbite Ridge?"

"Oh, I know this one!" Quigley shouted. "Because it's the fastest route out of Rookeryville. See, me and Jackson have tried all the escape routes from Rookeryville, just in case we ever have to chase a criminal, and the one over Frostbite Ridge is definitely the fastest."

Jackson nodded. "And don't forget Icejob will need somewhere to lie low until he gets his name carved on that cup. No one would look for him up there. Which is why we need to get a move on; we've got to stop him. Come on!"

"But how are you going to get up there?" Lily said, racing to catch up again.

"We're going to borrow the FBI's heli-hopper!" Jackson said. "I just need to find— Oh, excuse me, ma'am," he shouted to an FBI agent who was shuffling past, huddled under a black umbrella. "We urgently need to talk to Agent Bryn Rockflopper."

"He's in that tent over there," the agent replied. "But he won't see you. He and the boss are interviewing witnesses."

Jackson snorted. "Come on," he said to his buddies. "Of course he'll see us."

Lily frowned. "Do you really think the FBI is going to lend you their heli-hopper?"

"Sure!" Jackson said. "This isn't just a case of missing jewels and golden cups. There's a baby penguin in danger. Oh, hi there," he said to the two agents standing guard in front of the tent. "I'm Jackson. My uncle is an agent with the FBI. He's inside this tent and I urgently need to talk to him."

"Sure, and my uncle is a giant warty-walrus!" The stockier of the two penguins folded her flippers and sighed. "Go away, and stop bothering us."

"But this is important," Jackson said. "My Egg is missing and—"

"Lost toys are not FBI business!" The other penguin blew a gum bubble and popped it, spraying spittle in Jackson's direction. "Now scram!"

"Jackson's Egg isn't a toy," Lily said. "It's real, and it's been accidentally taken away by the penguin who stole the jewel."

"Yeah, yeah, I know, along with three umbrellas, a picnic hamper, and a pair of very expensive eyeglasses." The stocky penguin rolled her eyes. "Today everyone thinks the stuff they've mislaid has been stolen by whoever's got the jewel. Now get lost!"

Before Jackson could argue, a sudden gust of wind blew the tent flap open, and its occupants were revealed. "Uncle Bryn!" Jackson was about to shout. But before he could get the words out, he noticed the other penguins sitting next to his uncle. He gasped, then ducked his head and turned away. "Um—no problem. Thanks anyway," he mumbled. "Come on, guys. Let's go."

"Wait—what about the heli-hopper?" Quigley called, chasing after him. "I thought we were going to ask your uncle."

"We can't!" Jackson hissed. "Didn't you see who else was in the tent? Mrs. Heckle-Flipper and the Mom Squad! They must have been giving their witness statements. If Mrs. Heckle-Flipper hears I've lost the Egg, she'll call Mom!"

Lily sighed. "Maybe *you* need to call your mom, Jackson. This is getting serious."

Jackson shook his head. "No way! But don't worry," he said, his throat feeling drier than a hatchling's sandbox. "See, I've just decided that I'm going to get the little guy back myself. Because it's my fault it got lost." He shook the thick snow off his crest and began striding away.

"Wait for me!" Quigley said, setting off after him.

"*Stop!* You're both crazy!" Lily shouted. "It's too dangerous. I can barely see you through the snow. Let's go speak to those two agents again. We'll show them that TV footage." She glanced around the emptying field. "That news crew must be here somewhere."

But Jackson didn't look back. Head down, flippers pumping, he zoomed through the snow as fast as he could, with Quigley slipping and sliding behind him. But then— "Ahhh!" Jackson suddenly disappeared.

"Jackson? *Jackson?*" Quigley peered through the blizzard. "Hey—I see you. Grab a flipper!" And he hauled his buddy out of a large drift.

"Thanks!" Jackson shook the snow from his feathers. "This would be a lot quicker if we had a giant snowmobile."

Quigley cocked his head to one side, his gaze shifting from Jackson to the museum. "Wait—maybe we've got something better! Come on, I'll show you."

"**You've got to be kidding.**" **Lily gazed at** the giant mammoth, which Jackson was now shimmying up the side of.

"Quigley's right. It's perfect!" Jackson called down. "The ultimate snowmobile."

Quigley, meanwhile, was in a huddle with his cousin, Sunny, looking at the mammoth's control panel. "So the tracker app should now be connected to the mainframe of the mammoth, right?"

"Yep!" Sunny tapped a few more buttons on the controller and nodded. "Wherever that little Egg dude is, the mammoth will find him."

"Awesome. Thanks, Sunny!" Quigley gave his cousin a high-flipper, then scrambled up to join his buddy.

Lily shook her head. "I can't believe you guys are actually going to take this thing outside."

Sunny grinned at her. "It's what it's built for: ice, snow, chasing escaped criminals up freaky frozen glaciers!" He laughed, then lowered his voice. "But we're gonna need your help with those." He pointed to two enormous glass doors at the far end of the hall, which the museum used to move exhibits through. "We'll have to open them up fast, because when the security penguins see what's happening, they're not gonna be pleased."

"Aren't you worried you'll get into trouble?" Lily asked.

Sunny shrugged. "Well, this is kind of my fault. See, I accidentally sold some equipment to this bad dude who stole the jewel. And anyway, *Trouble* is my middle name."

"That's true," Quigley whispered to Jackson. "Sunny climbed out of his cot when he was three days old, and his parents found him with a screwdriver, taking apart the TV. They nicknamed him Trouble, and it kind of stuck."

"Um—guys," Lily called as she followed Sunny toward the giant doors at the end of the hall. "I still think we should go talk to the FBI first. I'm sure if we showed them all the evidence, they'll send their heli-hopper up to Frostbite Ridge and—"

"Sorry, Lily," Jackson interrupted. "There's no time."

Quigley flipped a switch on the remote controller, and there was a sudden rev-ving sound from the mammoth's belly. The creature began to twitch and toss its head, its heavy tusks thudding on the floor. Several visitor penguins passing the plinth jumped at the noise.

"Don't worry," Sunny called to them. "We're just carrying out some—uh—routine maintenance. Though—um—ma'am, you might want to step back a bit from the plinth."

"Ready, 00Zero?" Quigley said, pulling down his goggles.

Jackson slipped on his secret-agent dark glasses and grasped a chunk of the mammoth's thick hairy coat in his flipper. "Yep, let's do this!"

Quigley shoved the controller's lever into the drive mode, and the mammoth lunged forward. Visitor penguins who had taken shelter in the museum from the storm scattered. Several screamed. One with a hatchling in a stroller zoomed for the exit. But most just stood there, rooted to the spot, their beaks open, their eyes wide, as the mammoth lumbered toward the doors.

Jackson shivered as a blast of icy flakes shot into the room. In the distance, an alarm began to sound. *Uh-oh!* He spun around and spotted the security-guard penguin from earlier rushing into the room. He nudged Quigley. "I think we need to go faster."

Quigley hit another button and the mammoth shot forward.

"Go, dudes!" Sunny shouted, hopping from foot to foot and beaming up at his creation. "Hey, cuz," he yelled to Quigley, "I think my next project should be making a real mammoth from DNA. What do you reckon?"

But Sunny's words were whipped away by the howling wind and snow. *Whoa, it's like being on the ultimate scary theme-park ride,* Jackson thought as they thundered outside, straight into a wall of stinging snowflakes that pummeled the breath out of him.

Quigley flicked another switch, and the mammoth tossed its head higher, giving them some shelter as they charged down the museum's road, heading straight into the eye of the storm and onward to the terrifying outline of Frostbite Ridge.

Not that they could see much of Frostbite Ridge. Jackson strained to see anything through the snow. He was pretty sure he spotted the TV news crew filming outside the museum. "Hey, Rita!" He tried to wave, but then a sudden jolt sent him flying up into the air. As he smacked back down, Jackson flattened himself against the mammoth's bouncing spine, trying to move with the creature rather than against it. *Got to use the Sticky Starfish Technique again*, he reminded himself, spreading out his body and willing his feathers to somehow sucker on. His bones rattled. His beak shook, and his eyeballs felt like they were ping-ponging around in his skull.

The mammoth was climbing now, and its back had become an almost vertical slope. He tried to hold on even tighter. Then he made the mistake of looking down. *Yikes, the snow's up to the mammoth's knees now! If I fall off, no one will ever find me!* Jackson had a sudden vision of being scooped up by a snow-plough-sled in six months' time, just a bag of frosty penguin bones held together by a backpack.

He shivered and thought about the Egg. *I hope you're safe inside Icejob's backpack, little buddy, or you'll be frozen solid, and I'm not sure even sticking you in the micro-flipper on the max defrost setting will help.*

And still they thundered on, climbing up Frostbite Ridge.

After what felt to Jackson like several

eons of clinging on, the mammoth suddenly veered right, and the blizzard instantly weakened. *Huh?* Jackson looked up and saw a large rock jutting out above them, which was giving them a little bit of shelter. Something else was different, too. "Hey—the mammoth's slowing down!" he shouted to Quigley.

His buddy peered at his cell. "Yeah, the tracker app says we're close."

"But I don't see Icejob," Jackson said. "I don't see anything and— Hey!" He nearly fell off as the mammoth suddenly came to a juddering stop. "What happened?"

Quigley wiped the falling snow off his ice-Phone screen. "We've arrived. The Egg is here."

"Where?" Jackson flipped up his glasses and looked one way, then the other. "I don't see it." He felt a hot flush of fear creep through his feathers. What if the Egg had fallen out of Icejob's bag and gotten lost in a snowdrift?

"Hey, I hear something," Quigley said.

Jackson listened, but all he could hear was the wind, howling and whistling, but then—"Yeah, I hear it. It sounds like someone shouting 'help,' but I don't see anyone."

"Do you think it's him?" Quigley whispered. "Icejob?"

Jackson felt a wiggle of hope in his tail. *If it is, then he might still have the Egg.* "Come on, let's go take a look."

They shimmied down the mammoth's side, and instantly, everything went white.

"Urgh!" Jackson poked his head out of a snowdrift, spitting flakes and ice from his beak. He scrambled up, shaking the snow off his feathers and shivering with cold. "Agent Q? Where are you?" Then he spotted the tip of a flipper wiggling in the snow. "Here! I've got you—"

"Oh, wow, thanks!" Quigley mumbled,

cracking the frost off his beak as his buddy tugged him out of the drift. "I nearly turned Popsicle."

"Listen," Jackson said. "I can hear that voice again. It's coming from over there."

They edged around to the front of the mammoth, holding onto its hairy coat and testing every foot before they placed it on the snow.

"That's weird," Jackson said, staring at the path in front of the mammoth. "It sounds like

it's coming from under the ground— Hello?"
he shouted. "Where are you?"

"Here!" a small, smothered voice called
back from near their feet.

Jackson crouched down and shuffled forward along the path, parting the snow in front
of him as he moved. A large chunk directly
ahead of him suddenly fell away, revealing—
"Ah!" He jumped back. "Icejob!"

The snow on the path in front of them had been covering a deep ice crack, and stuck inside, perched on a ledge and peering up at them, was the master criminal himself.

"H-h-hi f-f-fellas! Am I p-p-pleased to see you!" Icejob's feathers were frosty, his crest was stiff with snow, and his beak was chattering so fast he could hardly get the words out. But Jackson could still see the ice-crystal tattoo glinting in the light. "D-d-do you think you can g-g-get me out of here?" Icejob said. "Because I'm f-f-freezing my feathers off!"

Jackson glanced at Quigley.

"Wow," his buddy whispered. "We found him!"

Jackson flicked the snow out of his eyes and cleared his throat. "Um—Mr. Icejob, I'm arresting you on behalf of the FBI for stealing the Ice Dragon's Eye and the Golden Egg Cup."

"Oh, is that r-r-right?" Icejob sighed. "Well, g-g-good work, kids. You g-g-got me. I'll c-c-come quietly. Just g-g-get me out of here!"

Jackson looked at Quigley. *Could it be this easy? Was Icejob really going to give up without a fight?* "Um—Mr. Icejob," he said. "I also think you have something of mine."

"I d-d-do?" Icejob cocked his head.

"Yeah, my Egg," Jackson said, crossing his flippers for luck behind his back and willing it to be there. "See, I think it rolled into your bag when you were—um—well, when you were dressed as that grandma penguin."

Icejob chuckled. "Oh yeah, I r-r-remember you and your Egg. So b-b-bothersome! But I can't check for your e-e-egg while I'm stuck down here, because as you can see—" He tried to move his flippers, but they smacked against the walls of his tiny ice hole. "If you h-h-help me out, you can l-l-look in my b-b-backpack."

Jackson stepped back from the hole and huddled close to Quigley. "Don't suppose you've got a rope, have you?"

"Nah, but I guess we could make a flipper chain?"

It was one of the survival techniques they'd learned from the *Secret Agent Handbook*. To rescue a fellow agent without a rope, you got as many penguins as you could find, and you all linked flippers to create a living rope.

Jackson scratched his crest. "With only two penguins?"

"Sure," Quigley said, reaching for the mammoth's trunk. "I'll hold on to this—then if I stretch over to you—yep, grab my flipper and you can reach in and grab him."

"Worth a try," Jackson said, leaning as close as he dared to the slippy hole. "Mr. Icejob, take my flipper and we'll pull you out—*whoa*! Not so fast!— Hey!— Stop! Ahhh!" Jackson suddenly found himself being tugged into the hole by the weight of the master criminal. "Let go!" Jackson shouted. "I'm faaalliiing!"

Just in the nick of time, Jackson managed to shake off Icejob's iron grip and, with Quigley's help, scrabble back to safety. He edged away from the crevice, panting and puffing, his heart pounding like Finola's favorite kettledrum solo.

"S-s-sorry," Icejob shouted up. "I guess I'm a heavy-b-b-boned penguin."

"What are we going to do?" Jackson gasped. "There's no way we can pull him up."

"My cell!" Quigley said, wiping the snow off his icePhone. "We'll call the FBI and tell them we've found Icejob, and they'll send the heli-hopper and— Noooo!" he groaned. "Battery's just died."

"Hey, kids!" Icejob shouted up from the hole. "You'd b-b-better think of something f-f-fast, because I don't think I can stand on this ledge much longer. My l-l-legs are going numb. And if I f-f-fall, so does your Egg!"

Jackson felt the air rush out of his lungs. He collapsed against the mammoth's trunk, trying to breathe, trying to think of something. Then suddenly, he turned and stared at the mammoth's trunk. "Quigley! Could we use this as a rope? It's long enough, right?"

"Oh, yeah, it's six feet at least. And it's made of carbon fiber," Quigley went on. "Which means it's ten times stronger than steel and—"

"Awesome, Agent Q!" Jackson interrupted. "Let's do this!"

Quigley pressed the controller, and the mammoth let out a loud bellow and his trunk thrashed against the ground, making the path shudder and chunks of snow and ice tumble off the rocks.

"Hoi!" Icejob growled, ducking as some dagger-shaped icicles dropped into his hole.

"Are you k-k-kids trying to start an avalanche?"

"Sorry!" Quigley muttered. "I'll mute the sound-FX mode."

"Mr. Icejob," Jackson said, leaning as close to the hole as was safe. "We're going to lower a kind of rope to you. Well, it's actually a woolly mammoth's trunk."

"I d-d-don't care what you send d-d-down," Icejob snapped. "Just get me out!"

Quigley hit another button, and the mammoth's trunk began to wriggle forward like a chunky snake.

"Right a bit," Jackson called. "Left a bit. Yep, that's it. Now lower it down."

"W-w-what the—festering feathers! This thing's weird," Icejob muttered. "But, okay, I've got ah-h-hold of it. Pull me up!"

Quigley pressed another button and the trunk began to lift. Seconds later, Icejob's head appeared at the top of the hole, his eyes

darting around, followed swiftly by the rest
of him. He jumped off the trunk and slunk
away from the crevice, shaking the snow and
ice off his feathers and stretching out his flippers. "Oh, that was too long! W-w-way too
long," he groaned, twisting his neck left then
right, then left again until it clicked.

Jackson coughed. "Um—Mr. Icejob, we'll
be leaving in a moment to go find the FBI."

He swallowed a few times, trying to sound confident, like a real secret agent, which was tough when your stomach seemed to have turned to cheesecake. "But before we leave—um—please, can I get my Egg now?"

Icejob stopped stretching and stared at Jackson, his eyes narrowing. "Oh, yeah, sure, kid." He slipped off his backpack and looked inside. "The FBI, eh?" he muttered to himself softly. "Mmmm, we'll see— Oh yeah," he called to Jackson. "Here's your Egg. No wonder this was so heavy!"

Jackson grabbed his soon-to-be-sibling, the relief washing over his feathers. He hugged the Egg, squashing his face against its cold shell. "I am so, so sorry, little buddy," he muttered. "I promise I won't lose you ever again— Hey, Quigley—it just did that shell stretching thing again. See? I really think it's going to hatch soon."

But Quigley was staring at Icejob. "Um— Jackson—look!"

Icejob had crept farther away from them now and was fiddling with something by his feet.

"Skis!" Quigley hissed. "Extendable sports skis! They must have been in his backpack."

Jackson lunged forward to try to stop him and nearly slipped into the crevice.

"Careful, fella." Icejob laughed. "You and your Egg do not want to end up scrambled down there." While he spoke he pulled out two extendable ski poles from his backpack.

"Stop!" Jackson growled. "You're under arrest."

Icejob snorted. "I don't think so. See, that trophy belongs to me. I lost the Games once. I'm not losing again! You boys enjoy your mammoth ride back home. Bye-eee!" He dug his ski poles into the snow to push off.

Jackson spun round, looking for something, anything, to stop him. Then he saw it. "Quick, Agent Q!" he yelled. "Use the mammoth's trunk as a lasso!"

His buddy didn't need asking twice. Quigley tapped the remote control, and the mammoth let out a loud bellow and lunged forward, its huge trunk shooting out and grabbing Icejob around the middle.

"Hoi!" Icejob squealed. "Gerrr-offf-meeee!"

As he tried to break free, the ground under their feet began to shake, and chunks of snow and ice started to fall off the rocks around them.

"Avalanche!" Icejob howled. "I told you that hairy beast machine would start one. And it's all your fault!"

Jackson stared up into the sky, blinking the snowflakes out of his eyes. "I don't think it's an avalanche. I think it's a—heli-hopper!"

Quigley looked up, too, a slow smile spreading across his beak. "Yep, an FBI heli-hopper, to be exact. I'd know that rotator sound pattern anywhere."

"The FBI?" Icejob's face turned pale. "Noooo! Let me go! I'll pay you."

Jackson's eyes popped. "Are you trying to bribe us?"

"Yep—you can have the sapphire, the cup, all of it!" Icejob tried to wriggle free of the mammoth's trunk. "Just let me go!"

"Sorry, Mr. Icejob," Jackson said. "Your escape plans have just melted."

"Yep, quicker than a snow cone in a micro-flipper!" Quigley laughed. He pointed to the flat ridge above them. "Look! The heli-hopper's landing."

Moments later they heard a shout, and then a group of penguins on skis came into

view, whizzing down the path toward them.

"It's Uncle Bryn," Jackson said. "And that looks like his boss and— Watch it!" he called to the group. "There's an ice crack just in front of us."

The penguins skidded to a stop, their eyes ping-ponging from the mammoth to Icejob to Jackson and Quigley to the Egg, then back to the mammoth again.

"Exploding icebergs," Uncle Bryn muttered. "You boys really did climb Frostbite Ridge on a woolly mammoth to rescue the Egg and capture Icejob!"

Senior Agent Frost-Flipper let out a long, low whistle. "And that's something you don't see every day. Well done, boys. I'm proud of you. The FBI could do with agents like you."

Jackson glanced at Quigley. Had they actually done it? Had they finally landed a job with the FBI?

Before Jackson could ask her, Senior Agent Frost-Flipper turned to Icejob. "Custard Dorkfin, also known as Icejob, you're under arrest for suspicion of theft. You have a right to keep your beak shut, to say nothing. But if you do say anything, it may be used in a Flipper Court against you. You have the right to an attorney penguin and—"

"Blah, blah, blah!" Icejob interrupted, poking his tongue out at her. "Button it, Frost-Flipper. I've heard it all before."

The FBI boss rolled her eyes. "Take him away, Agent Rockflopper."

"Sure, ma'am," Uncle Bryn said. "Um— guys," he whispered to Jackson and Quigley, "do you think you could unravel him, please?"

Half an hour later, Jackson and Quigley were inside the FBI heli-hopper, soaring back down to Rookeryville.

"This is awesome," Jackson murmured,

staring out the window as the lights of the town came into view.

Icejob let out a loud *harr-umph!* from the seat behind him. "Yeah, *really* awesome," he growled. "Utterly flipper-tastic!"

Quigley leaned forward and tapped Senior Agent Frost-Flipper on the back. "Excuse me, ma'am, but you'll definitely get someone to return the mammoth, right? It's just, the security penguins at the museum might notice it's missing, and I don't want to get Sunny into trouble."

"Might notice?" Senior Agent Frost-Flipper chuckled. "*Everyone* knows the mammoth's missing!"

"Everyone?" Jackson suddenly had a wobbly Jell-O feeling in his feathers.

"Sure! You two are famous!" Senior Agent Frost-Flipper said. "The news channel has been covering your story live on TV ever since you stole the mammoth and went off to rescue your Egg and arrest Icejob."

"Um—technically we *borrowed* the mammoth," Quigley corrected. "You see, Sunny said it was okay and—"

"Wait—" Jackson interrupted, suddenly feeling sweaty. "Did you say we were on the news?"

Uncle Bryn, who was sitting next to Icejob, leaned forward. "Yeah, your friend Lily and a camera-penguin called Rita showed us the news footage of the Egg rolling into Icejob's backpack."

"And Lily explained how you boys had found out about Icejob's disguises," Senior Agent Frost-Flipper added. "And how he stole the jewel *and* the cup. Nice work, boys."

"Oh please!" Icejob snorted from the back. "Nice work? What about me? I stole that sapphire from right under their beaks. And that

Golden Egg Cup should be mine! If I hadn't fallen into that ice hole, I'd be coming back as mayor."

"Zip your beak, Icejob!" Senior Agent Frost-Flipper snapped. "That woolly mammoth would make a better mayor than you." She turned back to Jackson and Quigley. "You boys are heroes. Look down there." She pointed out the window. "There's a welcome party waiting for you."

Jackson peered through the glass. He could see a large group of penguins standing in a huddle on the ground outside the museum.

"There's Lily!" Quigley said, jabbing his flipper against the window. "And Sunny and the head judge Wendy Webbingham and—uh—is that your mom?"

Jackson turned away from the glass. His feathers were standing on end. His legs had gone spaghetti and he seemed to have lost his voice. "Does this thing have a parachute?" he mumbled. "I might bail out early."

"Fasten your seatbelts," the pilot called. "We're about to land."

Jackson tried not to catch his mom's eye as he and Quigley climbed out of the heli-hopper. But Marina Rockflopper was already striding toward them, her face twisted like a Tiger Shark with a toothache.

But before she could reach them—

"Jackson! Quigley!" Bill Feathers, the TV
news reporter, dodged in front of her, with Rita
the camera-penguin right behind. "You're live
on TV," Bill Feathers said, his voice friendly
and smooth again. "Can you tell the folks at
home how you caught Icejob single-flippered?"

Jackson blinked under the bright camera
lights. "Um—well, we didn't do it all our-
selves."

"No, my cousin Sunny helped," Quigley
said, waving to him in the crowd. "See, he
built this awesome mammoth machine."

"And Lily helped, too," Jackson said, pointing her out to the camera. "She told the FBI where we were."

Rita spun her lens around and zoomed in on Sunny and Lily, who were both red-faced and smiling.

"What heroes!" Bill Feathers said as the camera turned back. "And tell us, Jackson, is it true Icejob kidnapped your Egg and that's why you had to go find him?"

Jackson winced. "Well—not exactly." He could see his mom glaring at him over the TV reporter's shoulder. "See, the Egg actually rolled into Icejob's backpack when I wasn't looking. But we got it back, safe and sound—look—" Jackson slipped off his backpack and pulled out his soon-to-be-sibling.

"My Egg!" Jackson's mom darted past Bill Feathers and grabbed it out of Jackson's flippers.

"Aw, folks," Bill Feathers said, beaming into the camera. "Isn't it lovely to see a family reunion. Hey—*Jackson's mom*, can we have a few words?"

"Oh yes!" his mom said, a sub-zero expression on her runny beak. "I've definitely got a few words to say to Jackson!"

He closed his eyes. This was it. He was about to get a Force-10 head-chewing, crest-blasting, feather-spinning telling-off LIVE on TV!

But before Marina Rockflopper could say anything, there was a sudden cracking sound.

"The Egg!" Jackson gasped. "Mom! It's hatching!"

"**W**hoa!" Quigley whispered. "Even Icejob couldn't come up with a distraction plan like that."

All eyes were on the Egg now as it began to shake and twitch in Marina Rockflopper's flippers. Small pieces of shell were cracking and falling into the snow.

"I can't believe this is happening live on TV," Jackson whispered to Quigley.

His buddy grinned. "Your family is going to be so famous."

Just then, a tiny beak broke through the

shell, followed moments later by a small gray head.

"Oh my word—I think—yes, I'm pretty sure—it's a girl, folks!" Bill Feathers shouted. "Congratulations, Mrs. Rockflopper! She's beautiful!"

And then suddenly everyone was cheering and clapping and congratulating Jackson's mom—and him! And for once, Marina

Rockflopper was speechless. She just stood there, staring at the tiny chick sitting in her flippers.

"Pardon me." Wendy Webbingham stepped forward. "I have some more good news to share. Jackson and Quigley," she said, turning to the boys, "the other judges and I have been following your daring rescue of your sibling-to-be, and we've decided you've both displayed *all* the qualities that Pip Rookery, the founder of our town, demonstrated all those years ago: bravery, kindness, and a desire to help others. We've also noted the bravery of your egg. Had she not rolled into the thief's backpack, we'd never have recovered the Golden Egg Cup, and for that reason, we have chosen all three of you to be future mayors of Rookeryville."

Huh? Now it was Jackson's turn to be speechless.

Quigley's face had turned the color of a seaberry. "Um—thanks," he said. "Only, we're actually going to be secret agents working for the FBI and—"

But no one heard him over the noise of the crowd whooping and cheering.

Wendy Webbingham raised her flippers for quiet. "We'll carve all your names on the cup today. Of course, we'll need a name for the new little hatchling." She looked at Jackson's mom.

"I—well—um—" Marina Rockflopper shrugged. "I don't really know. Any ideas, Jackson?"

The name popped into his head instantly. "Pip," he said. "Just like Pip Rookery!"

Everyone looked at his mom. No one moved. No one spoke. Then—

"Yeah." She nodded, a smile on her beak. "I like Pip. Good work, Jackson."

As more yelling and cheering erupted, Jackson nudged Quigley. "Hopefully if the chick is named after the founder of Rookery-ville," he whispered, "it might make her want to be mayor. Then we can be FBI agents instead."

"Awesome plan, 00Zero!" Quigley said, giving him a high-flipper.

EPILOGUE

"**A**re you wearing Finola's flip-flops?" Jackson gasped. "If she sees you, she'll go Great White!"

Hoff Rockface snorted. "Well she's not here, so who cares?!" He yawned, scratched his crest, then helped himself to another krill cookie from the tray Jackson's dad had just laid out to cool in the kitchen.

"And stop taking the cookies!" Jackson said. "Dad made them for Finola, not you."

Hoff burped and helped himself to another. "Just because I'm your servant,

Sweet-Beak," he said, "it doesn't mean you can treat me bad."

"*Me* treat *you* bad?" Jackson groaned. "You've got to be joking! You haven't lifted a flipper to help all morning."

It was a week after the Golden Egg Games excitement, and Hoff Rockface had come around to fulfill his side of the deal, to be Jackson's servant. But Hoff's idea of helping around the house was to lounge about, playing Jackson's Icebox and scarfing down all the snacks.

"Got any ice cream?" Hoff Rockface asked, shuffling toward the refriger-flipper.

"No!" Jackson blocked the way. "And even if we did, we don't eat ice cream at ten in the morning. My mom would go Hammerhead!" He looked at the clock. "She'll be back with Finola any minute, and we haven't even taken the garbage out yet!"

Hoff shrugged. "Go ahead, get busy, *Sweet-Beak*. I'll just have another cookie." As he reached for the tray again, a sly smile appeared on his beak. "Of course, if you don't want my help, I'm sure we can come to some sort of arrangement."

Jackson frowned. "What sort of arrangement?"

"Financial!" Hoff said. "Give me your allowance and I'll go home. Deal scrapped."

"What? Pay you to stop being my servant?" Jackson shook his head. "No way!"

"Suit yourself." Hoff squashed another cookie into his beak. "Mmm, not bad," he mumbled, spraying cookie crumbs all over the counter.

"Stop! Okay, I'll go find my wallet." Jackson slunk off to his room. *One minute I'm a celebrated secret-agent hero* and *TV star, not to mention a future mayor of Rookeryville, the next I'm giving Hoff Rockface all my allowance just to get rid of him.* Jackson sighed. Things had been going so well. His mom hadn't even reached Basking Shark on her Shark Scale of Crossness over the whole lost-Egg-mammoth-riding-FBI-criminal-chasing-in-a-blizzard-up-the-top-of-Frostbite-Ridge thing. She'd been so excited about Pip hatching, she'd forgotten to issue any punishments. Although when Senior Agent Frost-Flipper had suggested Jackson and Quigley might make great junior FBI agents, his mom had still managed to give "that look"—the one that stopped all conversations dead in their tracks.

Jackson pulled out his backpack from under his bed and began rummaging for his wallet. But just as he found it, he heard the front door burst open, and the sound of footsteps in the hall. *Finola?* Jackson froze and waited for the—scream! Yep, there it was. And it definitely wasn't Finola doing the screaming. Jackson grinned—this was about to get interesting. He dropped his wallet and raced into the living room.

"Whatdoyouthinkyou'redoing?!" Finola's beak was pressed hard up against Hoff's. "You are wearing *my* flip-flops!" she growled. "You're sitting in *my* seat. And you're eating *my* favorite cookies! Grrrrrrrrrr!" Finola plucked her drumsticks out of her crest. "If you don't leave right away, I'm going to use *you* for drum practice!"

Jackson had never seen Hoff move so fast.

"Hello?" Jackson's mom poked her head around the door. "Did Hoff leave already? I thought he'd come to hang out with you, Jackson?"

He shrugged. "I guess something came up."

Finola flopped onto the sofa with a cookie in each flipper. "Want me to hold Pip for you, Mom?"

At the sound of her name, Pip poked her head out of her hatchling carry-sack on her mom's back and squeaked.

"She's *sooooo* cute!" Finola cooed.

Jackson rolled his eyes. Why did everyone go ga-ga over Pip? As far as he could see, she was just a dribbly, stinky, annoying little blob who made *way* too much noise, usually in the middle of the night when most decent penguins were trying to get a little shut-eye!

Just then, the doorbell rang.

"I'll get it," Jackson said.

Pip's eyes followed him out of the room, and as soon as she lost sight of him, she started to wail.

Jackson heard his mom sigh. "Hush, Pip! Come on now. He'll be back in a moment— Pip's got a bit of a thing about Jackson," she told Finola. "She likes to be with him all the time. And whenever she can't see him, she starts squeaking."

"Really? That's weird," Finola said. "I'm the complete opposite."

Jackson snorted. "The feeling's mutual," he muttered as he opened the door.

"Jackson!" Quigley puffed, standing on the doorstep, panting and sweaty. "I—I—I came as fast as I could . . ." He paused to catch his breath. "It's the FBI r-r-radio," he said, hauling it out of his backpack. "It's started bleeping again. Listen!"

Calling all agents, calling all agents! A suspicious-looking submarine has been spotted approaching Rookeryville Docks. All agents respond immediately.

"What are we waiting for?" Jackson said. "After all, we're practically part of the FBI team now. Senior Agent Frost-Flipper as good as told us we were hired."

"She did?" Quigley cocked his head to one side.

"Well—almost. She was going to, then Mom gave her the look," Jackson said. "Wait there. I'll grab my backpack." But as he turned to go, his mom appeared with Pip in her flippers.

"Oh, hi, Quigley." She smiled. "Come on in—and Jackson, honey, would you boys mind playing with Pip while I make her some crab-mush for dinner? Finola's taking a bath and—"

"But, Mom!" Jackson wailed. "We were just about to go out and—"

His words were drowned out by Pip's squealing.

"Oh look how excited she is!" His mom's face had gone all soft and floppy. "See how she's holding her flippers out, Jackson? She loves spending time with you. There you go, little one," she added, handing the wriggling, dribbly little bundle to him. "I think you two are going to be great buddies, inseparable!"

Jackson glanced at Quigley and groaned. "Oh brother," he muttered, staring at the fluffy chick in his flippers. Their mission to join the FBI just got a hundred percent harder.

ACKNOWLEDGMENTS

Community is at the core of the Spy Penguins series. And so, too, for me, when I'm writing about Jackson and Quigley.

Thank you to the wonderful community of Feiwel and Friends, especially to my editor, Holly West, for her wisdom, guidance, and fantastic sense of fun. And also to the wider team at Feiwel and Friends; Spy Penguins wouldn't exist without you.

Thank you to Marek Jagucki, the immensely talented artist who brings the world of Rookeryville alive with his amazing pictures.

And also a heart-felt thanks to my awesome agent, Gemma Cooper, for the endless energy and encouragement.

My family is my world. Without them, I'd never achieve anything. Thank you to my rock-steady, unflappable husband, James, and my children, Alice and Archie, for their steadfast support.

And finally, I'd like to pay tribute to my mum, Shonagh Hay, who has always encouraged me to aim for the stars. Thank you, Mum, for the inspiration, the selfless love, and endless hugs. You're peng-tastic!